The Run

Alana Dyer

The Run

Alana Dyer

Published by Alana Dyer, 2023.

ISBN-13: 978-1-7381004-2-2

Cover design by: New Moon Covers

Library of Congress Control Number: 2018675309

Printed in the United States of America

This novel is dedicated to all the women who want to find their own true love. Stay strong my Queens!

Chapter 1 Grace

———

*T*he soft breeze rolls past me, ruffling the heavy gown that is draped on my small frame while I stare out into the field of moon flowers. The forest is alive with the sound of the creatures of the night. Quiet but still expressing the life it held within.

A soft touch moves my attention to the long golden hair tied with a ribbon, as a smile graces my lips. Finally, he is mine. My mate. The full blue moon illuminates the sky as I lean in to kiss the man I love...

My eyes quickly open as the dream, still fresh in my memory, haunts me. The gown that women wore with the corset bodice and flowing layers of fabric is something from a long, long time ago. I have seen dresses like that in movies and medieval dramas. I sigh, thinking how I have been having these dreams since turning eighteen two years ago. How a woman and a man would appear under the moonlight and silently display their love. How the woman in my dreams has my silver hair that flows down to her knees, and the man with long golden hair that is always tied out of his way. I wonder what these dreams mean and if it has something to do with The Run.

I can't help but turn my head towards the window beside me. The moon stared back down at me as if mocking me. It's as if the Moon Goddess is watching what I am doing, knowing that it will soon be the week of the blue moon, the week for The Run. I hated it, dreaded it. An event created over a thousand years ago, when the first werewolves were created by the Goddess herself. An event for wolves to run through a forest and be claimed and mated. But the truth is that it's just a way to approve of rape under the disguise of mating and growing a pack's strength.

In a few days, I will be sent to the Moon Goddess's forest when the full moon turns a brilliant hue of blue. But the truth is, I did not want to run through a forest of wolves, the females dodging males as they run for their freedom. I did not want to be forcefully claimed like my mother was. Never knowing if the male that took me as his mate - a male who just finished raping me in the Moon Goddess' forest - is going to be good to me and will give me a life of pure happiness, or will abuse me and create an even worse hell than I already live in.

I want a chance to fall in love. I want to go on dates and build a future with someone deserving. I want a male who would bashfully smile at me before leaning in for my first kiss and holding me close for the rest of our lives. I want my life to be mine and to have love that would last forever.

"Grace?" I snap out of my thoughts of self-pity and turn to look at all the wolves in the room, realizing that the Alpha is directing his statement to me. His eyes held annoyance at the fact that I had stopped paying attention to him. If a male had done this, it would have been fine. But I am a female. I have to sit quietly and listen to the males as best as I can in this pack.

"Sorry, I dozed off." It isn't a lie since snores from other wolves – male wolves- echoed the quiet room in this long meeting that the Alpha, the Beta - my father- and the Theta –our third in command- called forth for the mate-less wolves eighteen or older in Silver Birch to remind them that they will be taking part in The Run and the rules we are to follow.

"As I was saying, The Run is filled with multiple threats." My father continues, sending me a glare. I suppress the snarl rising in my throat and try my best to pay attention as the other wolves snicker behind me.

"Eli, the head of the Vampire Coven in that area, already alerted every Alpha that rogue fledglings have escaped before being welcomed into the coven and will be hunting for fresh blood to drink. He asked us to pass this message along to our members, so when you all are in the forest, keep your eyes alert." He announces, a frown on his face as he looks to the Alpha. Closing my eyes for a moment, I think back to my father ranting on about Vampires and how they should be killed while in one of his drunken stupors. Vampires were once our mortal enemy, as they were created by the Sun God out of boredom. It led to the goddess creating us wolves to keep the Vampires in check and protect the balance between the supernatural and the mundane world. Wars raged on for years, with many lives being lost. The most tragic event was the Salem Witch Hunt, where anyone deemed unnatural by the scared humans were hunted and killed, whether they were Vampires, Witches, Werewolves, Fae, or Humans.

It wasn't until a temporary treaty was signed over two hundred years ago that peace finally settled amongst the supernatural worlds. Things still happen between our two species that cause much uproar – including the Vampires instigating the humans to cause two world wars for the Vampires to enjoy an endless buffet – but we have been able to keep our races hidden from the humans thanks to the treaty. Unfortunately for us, with the Fledgling escaping, there will be some trouble ahead. Fledglings, especially rogue ones, pose a threat to both our species. This year's event would be even more dangerous with Fledglings running wild at night. All species will need to keep an eye out for them, just in case they escape and make their way to a human city. We do not need a repeat of the Salem Witch Hunt scare.

"Let's not forget about the faeries that live in the Moon Goddess's forest, either. If you run into one, stay still and listen to them until an opportunity to escape arises. Faeries are known to teleport wolves into traps or into the arms of un-mated rogues like the Raggers if you anger or upset them in any way." Mitchel the Theta continues the warning, making those around me nervous, while I scoff and roll my eyes. Faeries - or Fairies as humans call them - are known to cause trouble for Werewolves, Vampires, and Witches. They are mischievous and childish and come in many forms, from human-like fae to pixies to halflings. If you angered one at all, it would spell your doom.

I am lucky that I never had a problem with them. A coven of faeries lived just outside my grandfather's pack – Ocean Heart – in Newfoundland. I grew up learning from the Fae and even met their Princess many times due to their close bond with Ocean Heart.

I remember running into the woods one day out of boredom and stumbling into Pixies, their butterfly-like wings mesmerizing me as a pup. To me, the Fae are my friends, and after a year of friendship, the Princess had given me a token when I turned eleven: a gold earring I wear in my cartilage that is inscribed with a Fae charm of protection. They even gave my friend Amelia the same token, as she also befriended the Fae during her visits to Ocean Heart with me as pups when her father wanted my friend out of the way. I will be safe from the Fae hidden in the forest when I enter The Run. I just hope that Amelia has managed to find a way not to be sent into the Goddess's forest with me this year.

Thinking about Amelia, I look around the room, the desks lining the hall like a classroom filled with three wolves each, as I try to find my friend. To my surprise, I find her missing from the meeting, and I wonder if her father has her locked away before we are meant to leave for the event. Goddess knows how much he dislikes her free-spirited attitude and the fact that she fell in love with someone from our pack before entering The Run.

"Now I have one main point to finish this meeting. Many of you pups have expressed your dislike of The Run." The Alpha states his voice, causing my attention to return to the front of the room, where I find his gaze landing on me.

"But it is a tradition since the first Werewolves were created by our beloved Moon Goddess." He continues with his tone, holding no room to dispute him.

"Either you wolves go willingly to The Run or we will force a shift on you and cage you until it's time for the event to start and the chase to be mated is in full swing." His eyes stay glued to my sapphire ones, his brow raised as if waiting for me to object to him. To the top-ranking wolves, I am a nuisance, the one she-wolf that always voices my opinion about this barbaric event, made to make females submit to a male and bow down to the rules set by their new mate and their packs.

I can't help the snarl that rises past my lips as I hold his stare with my own. Hate and disgust radiate off of me in waves as I stand abruptly and slam my fist to the table in front of me, a crack forming down the center, and I am thankful to be the only one sitting here.

"Who do you think you are?" I ask with rage seeping out of me. I can feel my blood boiling as I continue to stare at my Alpha.

"Do you think you have the right to play with our lives like some puppet master?" Firing another question, I watch as his calm eyes narrow into slits and a warning growl escapes his lips. I have just challenged his words.

"I am your Alpha, Grace. What I say goes." He states eerily calm.

"Yes, you are the Alpha for now!" I shout, scoffing when he growls.

"But we wolves deserve a chance to find love on our own. Not be sent to this barbaric event." I continue, my body shaking as the power of an Alpha boils inside me. I can see my Alpha slowly growing displeased by my outburst, by me challenging his words. I know he wants to skin me alive now, to make an example of me, but he won't harm me with The Run being close to happening. I catch my father glaring at me, his own fuming rage barely being controlled as I embarrass him in this meeting.

"You will do as I say, Grace." The Alpha bellows out, his anger imbued in his words.

"I will not! I am a woman of the twenty-first century and demand the right to choose my own path." I declare, wanting to rip the man before me to shreds.

"Grace Harvest, sit down!" The Alpha yells at me with a command in his voice. The hushed whispers quiet down till only a pin drop can be heard as the tension between the Alpha and me thickens to the point it can be sliced with a knife. Being born with alpha blood from my mother, the only daughter of two powerful alpha wolves, gives me the ability to be on par with any regular alpha I meet. I can withstand any command as long as I do not see an alpha wolf before me as my Alpha, and can even challenge them if I so desire due to their disrespect. The only exception is the Alpha King.

"I will not sit down!" I state calmly, crossing my arms over my chest.

"I am the heir to the Beta position of Silver Birch as well as the best warrior in this pack, and I demand the same respect as one of the top ranking." My voice is clear as I speak my words, no wolf daring to refute me. They all know that I am just below the Theta in terms of power. I am the best warrior this pack has seen, and Mitchel always requests me for missions involving taking down rogues or transporting the Alpha and Amelia to other packs for meetings and treaty signings.

My father and the Alpha snarl at me, Mitchel just letting out a scoff as he leans against the wall. My rage is growing with every breath, my claws extending from what once were my nails. The Alpha and the rest of the wolves can feel the challenge as I slowly begin to walk towards the wolf my eyes are locked onto. My feet stop just mere meters from him, enough room to attack the Alpha before me, but also enough to keep space between us. I can see the thoughts swirling behind his eyes as he calculates a way to get out of this challenge, one I will gladly issue if it weren't for the fact that his daughter is my chosen sister, a sister that I consider my Alpha and will follow her command without a second thought.

"If you want to be treated like any top-ranked wolf in this pack, then go to The Run and win your freedom." His voice is strained as the Alpha holds in his boiling rage and piques my interest.

"If you can make it to the lodge by the end of the week, where I will be waiting, then I will no longer send wolves who do not want to participate in The Run and will give everyone a choice." It is an offer I could never refuse since this gave everyone a choice. Made she-wolves an equal in this one topic and will give them a chance to reject going to this event. Every wolf in this room stares wide-eyed at the Alpha and me, disbelief making the smirk on my face grow. I know that my father is not happy with this arrangement - this bet – but since his Alpha spoke it, he will have to obey.

"Fine, I accept this bet, but if I win, my father and you will also have to step down for Amelia and me to take over as Alpha and Beta." I uncross my arms and wait for the Alpha to speak. He knows the chances of me winning are high. I see him think things over, his eyes glossing over as the Alpha links someone, most likely Amelia, before nodding and stretching his right hand to me. Before I can hold out my hand to shake his and confirm the bet, the scent of an omega reaches my nose. My body turns on reflex to dodge, but I am not fast enough as a needle is shoved into my shoulder, the liquid inside entering my bloodstream and acting fast. My bones begin the snap as a forced shift is placed upon me, fur sprouting through my skin agonizingly until I am left on the floor in a ball of pain.

"I accept your terms, and I'll be waiting for you at the lodge, Grace. Make it there un-mated and free, and you win the bet, but if you do get mated by the time you make it to the lodge, then I continue forcing wolves to go." The Alpha states as he prowls towards me, his posture already triumphant when he comes to a stop before my frame as omegas carefully carry my silver-furred body to a cage that will hold me until The Run.

"Until then, enjoy the Run." His voice is menacing, and I growl with the anger still coursing through my body at the realization that an Omega had snuck up on me. This must be who the Alpha had mind-linked seconds earlier. He must have given a few Omegas sprays to conceal their scent in case a powerful wolf spoke out of line. Go figure, he had a plan set.

Soon, darkness creeps along my vision as the pain of the forced shift causes me to fall into the dark slumber of unconsciousness.

Chapter 2 Caden

———

I lament as I stare out the large window in my father's office, watching pack members run back and forth as they ready themselves for The Run. I hate the idea of The Run. It's a barbaric way of claiming a mate, one I regret my ancestors agreeing to. Growing up, I remember watching males bringing home she-wolves and vowing that I would not rape an innocent she-wolf like they did, and instead find someone on my own terms and fall in love. But, as the next Alpha to my pack, I have to take a mate this time or face losing my title as heir and watch my power-hungry cousin take my place instead. Losing my title if I do not bring home a mate is something my father has been threatening me with for the last six months, since the last time The Run came around.

"Remember, Caden, you are the Heir to this Pack. Every wolf counts on you to claim a mate and produce the next round of heirs and pups. Do you understand?" My father's voice commands my attention, and I find myself looking away from the window and facing him with a stoic expression. The man screams Alpha with the way he walks as if everything and everyone is beneath him, including his own son. I know his question is rhetorical, and answering him will lead to a beating that will leave me unable to participate in The Run and consequently lose my position as his heir. His eyes look in my direction while I give a slight nod as a response, eyes cast down. It is pathetic to think I have to be this submissive to my father, but anything I say will be viewed as challenging his authority, and I know I need to play possum in order to take the pack from him forcefully when he least expects it.

"Good. You may leave." With a final nod of respect to my father, I silently leave the room and make my way down the corridors to the garage where my truck waits, praying I can leave before I run into anyone in my pack.

"Hey Caden, going to get a mate this time around, or am I finally going to take the spot of Alpha from you?" I bristle at the voice of a weasel as I look to my cousin Felix. The lanky five-foot-nine man with greasy black hair has a thin arm wrapped around a terrified girl. Linda's face is hidden behind her long blonde hair, but the shadows created by her locks can not hide the fact that her face is thin and bruised from years of abuse, and how she covers it with a layer of makeup to try and hide the black and blue spots left from fists. Her efforts in trying to hide the dark circles under her eyes, bruises on her cheeks, and the split lip that looks painful even from where I stand are in vain, as I can see them clear as day.

"Unfortunately, I have to take a mate the old-fashioned way." I glare at the man as I start placing items into my truck.

"But I will treat her with respect, kindness, and dignity. Unlike how you treat Linda." I growl out, narrowing my eyes at Felix as I throw my last bag into my truck. Linda flinches at the loud sound, shrinking farther into herself. I can't help the guilt at scaring the poor girl accidentally, as I give her an apologetic look before turning to study the man who shares part of my DNA. As the only son of my late Aunt, Felix takes after the man whom I used to call Uncle until he killed my Aunt in a fit of rage.

"What do you mean, Cade? I treat Linda fine, don't I, baby?" I watch as Linda's eyes gloss over with more fear than I have ever seen on a she-wolf while she nods her head slightly, pressing herself to her forced mate to appease him.

She is malnourished, with bones poking through the thin, transparent material that should have been her skin. Skin that barely had any clothing covering her with bruises, scars, and healing cuts on what was once full, supple, tanned skin. I remember meeting her years ago in her original pack. How full of life and dreams that a young girl at sixteen usually has. Now she is just a shell of fear and anxiety.

When I become Alpha, the first thing I am going to do is send Felix on a mission to supply the food storage for winter. I can already see the trap laid out as he aims for the biggest buck he finds, his eyes glazing over with the bragging he would do when he returns to the pack. The antler rack he would mount on his walls with pride, and then the shock when his eyes sees the red blossom from his chest and the realization he would bleed out and die in seconds because of a single silver bullet that was *accidentally* shot. I will enjoy knowing this scum died in an *accident*. Enjoy knowing his mate will be free and happy to do as she pleases. I would even send her back to her original pack and back to her family with enough money to live comfortably alone if she chooses.

"See, I treat her right." Felix gloats, digging his nails into her shoulder and snapping me from my daydream that I pray will be the future. I watch as Linda forces her spine to straighten, disgust flashing briefly on her face before her eyes meet mine with a question.

[Will you really force a Mate?] She asks through a link as Felix is distracted by an Omega with a thin waist and ample chest.

[No, I would rather not, and the truth is I have a plan. Can you hold out for another week?] My response brings a sparkle to her eyes, and she nods quickly. With a small smile, I turn to my cousin and growl at his obvious disrespect to me. I hate that this weasel ignores my presence most of the time and acts as if he is the next in line for the Alpha position.

"Don't do anything stupid while I'm gone, Felix. I don't want to deal with the after math in the end." I warn, my six-foot-two giving Linda a hug that I hope shows her everything will turn out for the better, frowning at the whimper of pain the light pressure brings, before I turn and walk to the driver's side of my truck and climb into the cabin. I catch Linda's hopeful gaze in the mirror before giving her a small nod and driving away. I have to help her.

I remember the year Felix claimed her. We had just turned eighteen at the time, and it was our first time entering The Run. At the time, I was naïve. Felix and I were like brothers since childhood, always playing and training together. He was my best friend, and we swore that we would not force a mate together just before leaving for the event. Then we entered the forest and everything went downhill fast. Felix caught the scent of Linda. The youngest daughter of the Beta of Greywind – a pack in Alberta - and his instincts to mate with someone stronger or of similar strength took over. By the time I managed to get to him, it was too late. Linda had a bloody mate mark on the crook of her neck, and Felix was grinning as he mercilessly raped her into submission.

It wasn't until those seven days of The Run had passed and we were resting at the lodge that I learned that my so-called father put the idea of Felix being Alpha into his head if Felix took a mate, and I did not by the age of twenty-four. That was the day I lost a brother, a cousin, and a best friend. That was the day Linda started being abused, and my hate for The Run deepened.

With a sigh, I put my truck into drive and begin the journey to the Goddess's Forest, where the event will be held. I just hope that maybe this year I could find someone who would date me before we mate.

It was wistful thinking, but it is the only hope I have right now.

Chapter 3 Grace

———

T he steady hum of an engine wakes me up from the solid darkness of sleep. The drugs that had numbed and weakened my limbs slowly fade from my system. With each passing minute, I am able to move just a little bit of my body at a time, starting with my tail, then my paws, until finally I am able to have full control of my body with just a little sluggishness in my limbs. I let out a long growl filled with anger as I think about the little trick the Alpha pulled with the Omega, pissed at the man who is supposed to lead our pack, and pissed at myself for letting my guard down. I should have been on high alert even within Silver Birch, as I am an eyesore to the Alpha. A she-wolf with an opinion is not one many males want to keep around.

The humming under my paws alerted me to the situation. I lay in a small cage barely big enough for me to move around in wolf form, but would be perfect for me in human form if it weren't for the drugs keeping me from shifting. Another cage is situated right against my own, but due to the tarp that covers mine and keeps me safe from most of the harsh elements, I can not make out the occupant beside me. With a deep breath, I focus on scenting the air to figure out who else fought against going to The Run until the scent of strawberries and pine -the familiar scent of Amelia, daughter to the Alpha of my pack – hits my nose.

I think I now know why Amelia wasn't at the meeting. I think sadly, as I stretch my limbs, happy to be drug-free. I want to see if Amelia is okay, if she was beaten by her father before being caged, but I am stuck inside my own prison and can barely see past the tarp. I am left to focus on my own stiff body at the moment.

It is pathetic, really.

The fact that they would cage a grown woman just to prove a point in the era we call the twenty-first century, where women have rights, disgusts me. Unfortunately, due to the way the packs are ruled by the Alpha King, I have no choice but to comply with the patriarchal ways of werewolf society. What I would give just to be human. To be able to live a more normal and free life. Even being a rogue would be a better option than being part of a pack, as rogues only show up to the event if they want to.

Taking a deep breath to calm my anger, many scents rush into my nose, and a smirk spreads on my muzzle with the realization of us being on the outskirts of my pack near the edge of the border; outside of it, to be exact. If I can knock this cage onto the ground, I will be set free and given a chance to run away and hide from the event that would take place soon for mateless wolves. With that thought in mind, I crouch, focusing on the center of the bars and leap forward, feeling triumphant until I touch the metal that greets me and howl with pain.

Silver.

Of course, the bars would be silver; it sadly is the Kryptonite to us werewolves. Silver is the only way to keep us locked inside the stupid cages or to harm us in any way, even kill us, sadly. Many Hunters who know of the supernatural races use silver to harm us and even kill us for rewards. It is something we feared – vampires, witches, fae, and werewolves alike.

With a whimper, I stand, shaking my fur out as the scent of burnt skin fills my senses. Quietly, I pad towards the spot I awoke in and sit in the center, waiting for when my cage will be opened, most likely at the start of The Run. Judging by the moon, tomorrow night will be when it takes place, sooner than I hoped, but sadly, it will happen no matter what.

[Amelia?] I call out through the link, trying to reach my best friend. I wait, receiving nothing but silence, and worry gnaws at me.

[Amelia, can you hear me?] I ask a little more frantically while looking towards her cage. The sounds of someone stirring beside me bring a slight relief, and I wonder if the dosage of drugs injected into her was higher than the one I received.

[Grace?] Her voice is weak, barely audible through the link, but Amelia soon reaches out, and I am relieved. Thank the Goddess she did not overdose on the drugs.

[Amelia, are you okay?] I ask, hearing a slight whimper in response.

[No. Alpha sent Bryden away on a suicide mission. I haven't eaten anything in days.] She answers, her voice slowly growing quieter. I suppress a growl, wanting to sink my teeth into the man who fathered her more than ever. Bryden is the man Amelia loves, the man she wants to mate with. The fact that the Alpha would separate them all because he wants his daughter to be claimed the old-fashioned way is disgusting.

[Go back to sleep, then, Amelia. Try to conserve as much energy as you can for now.] I coo to the she-wolf, wanting to curl around her and help take away her pain.

[Okay, Grace.] She meekly agrees before silence settles between us. I listen until my friend falls back asleep and sigh, sending a prayer to the Moon Goddess to help Amelia metabolize the drugs before we reach the event. Hopefully, she can get some form of food when we arrive, or else Amelia will be in trouble.

I let out a small huff of breath, I curl up into a ball and think of what I can do to win the bet and keep Amelia safe, watching the scene change through the small opening between where the tarp doesn't touch those damned silver bars. Looking out the bars of the cage, I take in the night sky and take a deep breath. I know just by looking out towards the night sky with an almost full moon, I had slept for a day, maybe two. It is easy to tell with the fresh scent of rain that still lingered in the air - rain that was forecasted the night of the meeting to be arriving by Tuesday morning. The night quickly gave way to morning as time passed; the indigo sky came alive with the hues of gold, orange, red, pink, and violet as the sun claimed its glory.

The Run waits for me silently to join in a few hours now, and if I want to win the bet with the Alpha, then I would have to rest and save my strength. So I let the safety of sleep surround my mind willingly, as whoever drove the truck carted me to the worst event ever.

One that may even change my life and fate if I allow it to.

Chapter 4 Caden

———

[M]ake sure you bring a mate, or else.] My father links me, a warning hidden in his voice, causing me to clench the steering wheel tighter as I leave the safety of my pack. The magic of the barrier hiding us from view passes over me, reminding me that my secret must be kept hidden when I drive through the human towns. I cannot let anyone know I am a werewolf until I reach The Run.

I hate the condescending tone my father uses towards me, knowing that he sees me as nothing but a useless wolf, even if I carry the same Alpha blood as he does, especially considering my mother was also a pure-blooded Alpha wolf when she was alive. I stop the truck as soon as I am a safe distance inside neutral territory and away from the pack line, taking a deep breath before my anger can slip through into the mind link. The last thing I need is an argument with my father, while still just in reach to be pulled back and beaten.

[Yes, sir. I understand.] I reply courtly once calm enough to communicate with this man. My body shakes with anger and rage as I roll down the window to allow the familiar scent of trees, dirt, and foliage to calm me. An angry wolf at The Run is a dangerous wolf, and I have witnessed one too many deaths caused by a stupid Theta or Warrior instigating a pissed off Alpha or Beta to look tough in front of the she-wolves until blood is splattered and screams of panic resound around the clearing. Where co-ordinators would have to separate the Alphas and Betas from the lesser wolves and sedate them for the safety of others. I have been one of these wolves once upon a time, when Felix had one of his cronies instigate me on my third trip to The Run, and the drugs used on me kept me weak for the whole week. I did not want to be put in that situation again.

I continue to take deep breaths, thinking about my sister and my kind mother as my anger slowly dissipates. I remind myself that this time things will be different. That in a few days, I will no longer need to deal with Gregory – my father – anymore once I make it to the Lodge in seven days. That, with my pack situated in the northern part of Ontario, nothing will attack them until I get back from The Run. My eyes flicker to the dashboard, and I press harder on the gas after realizing I may be late. Just another two hours on this road and I will reach the destination where The Run will take place.

The Run has been around since the original pack was created. The first Alpha King and leader of all wolves around the world created this event when she-wolves were created, as the females were considered a limited supply to the population of werewolves. The species needed to survive, and the strongest genes needed to be passed down, hence The Run and the claiming of a mate.

After the success of the first run, the tradition was carried down. Something about taking a female by force seemed like the ultimate manly thing to do, and during those time periods where the male had to be strong and their offspring stronger to survive made sense at the time. Unfortunately, this meant mateless wolves from around the world are forced to come to the Moon Goddess's Forest twice a year to find a mate when the moon is full and the colour is a deep blue, almost sapphire, because of the magic in the air.

I wish I did not have to go, but if I did not find a mate this week, then I would be forced to step down as the heir to my pack and let Felix take it. This will be a mistake, and the downward spiral he would create will be catastrophic to say the least. My grip on the wheel tightens even more as I clench my jaw. I will not let Felix steal my birthright; I will do everything to keep his power-hungry hands away from my pack and away from the pack bank account. I know Felix will ruin my pack and all werewolves will crumble under his reign if he were to become Heir.

With a frustrated growl, I pull to the curb and get out, kicking a nearby tree as I let out my pent-up anger. Anger at my father for continuing to force pack mates to The Run. Anger at the abuse the she-wolves face every day. Angry that I can do nothing until I take over and get rid of my Father.

After a few minutes of angrily attacking the sturdy tree till it was nothing but firewood, I stop, clenching and unclenching my fists until my breathing evens and I crack my neck. Stretching slightly, I walk back to my truck and drive away. I might as well get this done and over with and get back to my pack with a mate in tow. Maybe after the shock of being claimed, I can win her heart and give her a chance to see that I am actually a good man. That I will never harm her the way my father harmed my mother until she commits suicide to leave me.

Who am I trying to fool, though? If I had to force myself onto a she-wolf, then I would have already harmed her.

Chapter 5 Grace

———

The truck finally comes to a stop, and I lift my head, the sky slightly darker as the sun begins to set. By the smell of many wolves congregating together, I conclude that we have finally reached our destination - The Run. The engine is turned off as I watch wolves walk by the truck. Some call out to their friends while others walk over and peer under the tarps and into the cages that hold me and Amelia to see if we are good mate candidates. I can hear the she-wolf beside me growl at those curious to see who was held and can't help but frown. She should know by now that giving these men attention will cause them to want to break her.

[Amelia, calm the fuck down before some dumb ass decides he likes it rough and feisty.] I snap out through our link. She needs to be quiet, pretend not to care if she is to survive this event mateless.

[Sorry, Grace.] She responds with guilt in her voice. The growls beside me subside, and the air around us settles as Amelia takes deep, even breaths and slowly calms down. I know that when our cages are removed from the truck that we will be separated, a tidbit of information I gleamed on one of the rare stops the wolves driving the truck made. The Alpha wants to keep us from meeting up, from protecting each other, and making it harder to win the bet. But he has no idea we already have a plan we made years ago after one of the beatings Amelia and I received when we voiced our reluctance in going to the Run.

[Do you remember the cave we said we would meet up at in three days?] I ask my friend, carefully eyeing the wolves that come to sate their curiosity about us in the cages.

[Yes!] She answers quickly, making me smile in relief.

[Good. Meet me there. Your father and I have a bet, and I intend to win it with both of us being unmated.] I continue, getting a yip of approval. Her father would not want me to be at her side and would not want me preventing a strong male from claiming her and becoming the Alpha of her pack instead of allowing Amelia to take over. He knows I will put protecting Amelia over the bet, but the thing is, as much as I know I have to protect Amelia now, knowing that she was here as well, I also know Amelia is a strong fighter and will take down any male that stands in her way. As long as she stays away from the center of the forest and follows the plan we have created since our seventeenth birthday, she will make it to the lodge un-mated with or without me.

Hearing voices drawing near, I go on high alert, waiting to see who is coming up the side of the truck, and sigh, realizing it is two of my packmates who climb onto the back of the truck and make their way to the cage Amelia is kept in.

They work fast with their hands gloved to protect them from the silver while they remove both tarps covering our cages. Amelia sends me a look of fear as she is the first to be carried away to have the cage she resides in be placed at the starting line. Watching her being loaded onto a golf cart provided by event coordinators, I send her a reassuring look, reminding her through our link that we will find each other and we will come out un-mated. She has a boyfriend waiting for her back home and knows I would do anything to see them together in the end.

With my stomach growling, I wait silently for the men to return, noticing their mark-less necks earlier when they took Amelia away. These men are here to participate and were in charge of delivering Amelia and me. No doubt they did their best to keep her and me starving in order to weaken us and try their best at claiming the Beta and Alpha blooded she-wolves of the pack. Too bad for them, as I plan to keep the two of us mateless.

Finally, the men return, both laughing about how easy Amelia will be to take down, and I growl, ready to rip them to shreds for disrespecting our future Alpha like that.

"Just ignore her. I bet within a day, with how weak Grace is, she will be claimed instantaneously by a Beta, maybe even an Alpha." The brunet, a warrior named Mark, laughs out as he takes hold of the silver bars to my right.

"Honestly, I want to see her win the bet against the Alpha. I have a little sister who turns eighteen next year. I don't want her being raped." The redhead, Chris, states. My anger towards him diminishes and I look at him with a questioning glance, deciding to ignore Mark.

[I don't want to be here either, Grace. I am just keeping Mark in check. If he goes to rape someone, I will knock him out and allow the she-wolf to escape.] Surprised by Chris linking me, I lower my head onto my paws while my pack mates bring my cage to a golf cart and hop onto the empty seats. The drive is quick, and once again, the boys are back lifting my cage and carefully bringing me to a clear spot lined with a few cages already. Mark tries to poke at me, and I send him a warning snarl, ready to claw his hand apart if he tries anything. Chris thankfully pulls him away - reminding the idiot that I have on numerous occasions sent Mark to the infirmary for a month-long stay when he has pissed me off in training - and watch as the two walk away, Mark staring at me with slight fear.

With a puff of breath, I stop growling, realizing that all the growling I am doing is drawing unwanted attention from the more power-hungry wolves, the ones looking for a female they can break into ultimate submission. I refuse to be one of them.

With a flick of my tail, I close my eyes, playing indifference to the idea when in reality I want to go out and destroy all those males that stare at the she-wolves like a buffet ready for the taking. Like a commodity they can buy and do as they please to them. These are the wolves I will need to stay away from during my week in the forest.

There are still a few hours left before the blue moon will appear, just waiting till midnight when it will be at its highest peak. My nightmare will begin the moment the clock strikes twelve, and if I do not make it out as an unmated wolf, I will lose the bet and any chance at respect from the males in my pack.

"Hello, ladies and gentlemen." A voice calls the attention of all wolves to the center of the field between the starting line and the trees of the forest. A stage I had not noticed till now is set up with a screen displaying a man as the wolf waits for everyone's attention to be on him. If a stage is set up, that means something important is to be announced.

"Today, we have a special guest to explain some new dangers that have come up recently." The announcer states with his lips set into a grim line.

"Please welcome the Vampire Eli, the Ancient." Wolves clapped respectfully as Eli, head of the Vampire coven in Ontario, stepped forward and smiled down at everyone. His skin is as white as snow, but the sun did not harm him in the slightest. Courtesy of his age and tolerance he's built up over the years. I watch this man, studying and wondering just how strong this ancient vampire is and whether or not I can take him in a fight, even if it is a mock fight for training.

"I hope each of your Alphas informed you that many of my newly awoken vampires have taken refuge in the Moon Goddess's Forest before we could initiate them into the coven." Eli the Ancient begins with a sigh, his pristine face looking a little haggard on the large screen behind him.

"This was neglect on our fault. As such, if you see one, kill the rogue vampire without hesitation. They will be blood-deprived and feral as a result of running away and will attack anything with a pulse." He continues explaining, his face holding no smiles or smirks. Just a frown as his bright blue eyes display a weary and exhausted look. This man must be beating himself up on the inside for losing these rogues and letting them escape into the world before they can be trained properly. Thankfully, my pack was warned earlier this week. We already knew of the risk this year, and I am ready to face one and kill the fledgling if need be.

Eli continues to apologize for his negligence before explaining the many ways to kill a vampire fledgling, making sure we all know to decapitate them and leave their bodies in a sunny spot to burn away to ash. He did not want any to come out alive. This was a statement, a truth between the Vampires and Werewolves, with him permitting us to kill these newly awoken vampires.

"How many fledglings are loose?" Someone calls out once Eli has finished speaking.

"Ten. Four females and six males." The ancient answers, turning to the announcer from before.

"If there are no other questions, this man seems to have something to say." With that, we all watch as Eli vanishes from the stage, and the wolf from earlier returns to the podium and gives the crowd a friendly smile.

"It seems this year will be a bit more precarious. Please be careful when out in the forest. Once the barrier settles around the Goddess's Forest, no one will be able to leave unless it is to exit by the lodge." The announcer awkwardly states before reminding everyone of the rules, especially for those newly turned eighteen-year-old wolves participating for the first time.

I drift out of the conversation and focus on resting since I will need my energy for later tonight, as I already know the rules being she wolves will have a head start to enter the forest first. There are caves and dugouts we can hide in as long as we want, but we must make it to the lodge by the end of the seventh day at exactly midnight. There is no killing allowed in the forest; it is sacrilegious to the Goddess and can result in execution. No raping a claimed she-wolf if you stumble across one. They already bear a mark. If a she-wolf is to be raped by a man other than the one who marked her, then the mating will be null and void, and the mark will fade within a day.

The wolf up on stage continues to talk, and I decide that I need to improve my plan for this event. If vampires are roaming around, then I have more than just males thinking with their dicks to deal with this year.

As I think about what I will need to do to guard against these vampires more, male wolves start to walk by the cages, sizing up the ones that try to break out of the silver cages and attack their onlookers, looking like feral beasts needing to be tamed. I just roll my eyes, silently laughing at how stupid these she-wolves are, as their actions only cause the strongest here to become interested in them. Many walk by me eyeing my silver fur, but losing interest quickly when they realize I am just curled up, resting and ignoring their presence. They mean nothing to me, and not drawing a male's attention is my plan.

"She's harmless..."

"Why is she even in a cage..."

"Let the weak ones have her..." I chuckle inwardly, listening to the criticism thrown my way by the males. They have no idea just what a force I can be. Have no idea that I sent the Theta's son, our top warrior, just after me, to the infirmary, just a breath away from death's door, all because he tried to rape me on my sixteenth birthday. If these males cross my path in the forest, they will learn just how lethal a warrior I can be. Another hour passes, and I doze in and out of sleep while the chatter of wolves still in skin form grows louder and louder as many inch closer to the starting line. The Run will begin soon.

Suddenly, the scent in the air changes, and the clearing quiets down. I open my eyes and smirk.

The moon begins to ascend into the sky, climbing higher and higher, signalling that the time is near. Co-ordinators of The Run – mated wolves whose job is to keep us safe – climb onto the cages keeping the problem females captive. They are waiting for the gunshot to release us.

Thankfully, the wind is blowing softly from behind us. I could not get any luckier with nature on my side. With my scent blowing away from the males and deep into the forest, I will be able to get away quickly and find a hiding spot that hopefully has gear or food for me to take. With a plan in mind, I slowly climb to my feet and lazily stretch, preparing my body to run because my life depends on it.

Taking a look at my surroundings, I count the number of cages I can see on my left, realizing I am the first in the long line that slowly fades after counting to fifty. Most she-wolves continue to growl and snarl at the males that eye them like a prize to be won, a pet to tame and claim as their own, and I roll my eyes again. The ones that lie there calmly or sit watching the forest with intent are the ones I know will survive unmated and make it safely to the lodge.

On my right are the unmated she-wolves still in skin form. The ones wanting to be here and gain themselves a mate that can take care of them, or are here to officially mark the man they have been sweethearts with for years. I can tolerate the ones here for love and making their relationship official, but the ones stretching in provocative ways - teasing the males behind them - are the ones I would rather claw apart than get to know.

Personally, I just want out of this cage.

Out of this event, and to gain the freedom to choose my own mate and live my life my way.

Deciding to face the forest, I focus on breathing and readying myself to run like the wind. Ignoring the noise behind and beside me. I can not afford any distractions right now.

As the moon continues to climb, the air around the clearing begins to hum. I have never participated in the run before - always being sent on missions just before the event was to start, as soon as I turned eighteen - so I never got to see the spectacle of how the moon turns blue. As such, when the air began to shimmer, I instinctively looked to the full silver moon high in the sky, just barely reaching midnight and in time to watch the magic unfold.

It started off like faerie dust, swirling in the air around the outer edges of the moon. A swirl of blue glitter that dances to a song silent to everyone else. Mesmerized by the swirls slowly covering the silver moon, I stare in awe as the seconds tick by and the silver fades away. That is, until a thin veil falls from the sky, the colour is just as blue as the magic covering the moon above. This veil surrounds the forest before us wolves, making the green trees appear a brilliant sapphire like my eyes.

The event will begin soon, and I reluctantly return my focus to the forest path before me. As pretty as the moon is, my safety and survival as an unmated wolf came first.

Five

The men shift above the cages, grabbing the lock while I count down the seconds until I am free.

Four

Male wolves changed as the sound of clothing tearing breaks the silence.

Three

The frantic growls of the caged she-wolves fill my ears.

Two

I take one last deep breath, closing my eyes and sending a silent prayer to the Moon Goddess that I make it out of the forest safely and un-mated.

One

The cage doors are released, and I open my sapphire coloured eyes, dashing out of the prison and into the forest. I am the first to reach the safety of the once green trees, but now glowed blue like the moon above, dodging and weaving around the sturdy trunks and making my way as quickly as I can to the sound of water.

Seven days for the full moon to be blue.

Seven days from the starting line to the finish

Seven days, that's how long I had to make it to the lodge as an unmated female.

Chapter 6 Caden

———

After a long drive and a detour to the nearest Tim Horton's for a much-needed coffee, I finally make it to the location of The Run. It looks like I just missed Ancient Eli's speech about the rogue vampires, judging by the time and the way the stage that was set up for the guest is being dismantled. Thankfully, my father gave me the information earlier in his office when he was berating me about bringing home a mate or losing my title.

I groan, thinking about the troubles newly awoken vampires can bring if they haven't been initiated into a coven or trained properly. Fledglings are nothing to take lightly, their bloodlust causing the fall of many cities for centuries when careless vampires would turn humans in hopes of creating their own coven. World War Two is proof of that. I just hope that the wolves who manage to run into the fledglings can swiftly take care of them, and no harm will come to the weaker wolves.

With careful driving, I manoeuvre my truck around the parking spaces provided for those who drove here like myself. Annoyed by the wolves that barely move out of the way of my truck. I think about what antics to expect this year, other than the fledgling. Last year, a group of rogues called Raggers kidnapped many omegas and rogue she-wolves – the weakest of attending females – and unfortunately, no one was able to find their base of operations in the forest, leading to a massive headache for the coordinators. In the end, many she-wolves were proclaimed missing when The Run came to an end, and all the Alphas were left feeling angered at the loss of females that could have grown their packs.

One of my goals this year is to find the place the Ragers hide and bring this to the coordinator's attention as quickly as possible so that a trap to capture them can be made.

Finally, I find a parking spot next to my pack mate, Zander, who waves nonchalantly at me. As I park and step out of my vehicle, the first thing that hits me is the scents of so many wolves in one area. With just a quick glance, I can tell the formation of cliques has already begun among those who arrived early.

Those of higher rank stuck together, staying closer to the front to eye the she-wolves up for grabs. Those who are weaker - like the Omegas- are careful not to get between the higher-ranked wolves and stay closer to the back of the wolves gathering if they are males. She-wolves stick to the very front, closest to the forest, and not to get in the way of the whores doing their best to gain the attention of the powerful males before them.

"You get volun-told to come here?" I ask my friend, walking over and hugging him.

"It was either come here or be forced on a suicide mission by your father. I think coming here is safer than dealing with Gregory." Zander answers, his eyes unfocused as he looks towards the forest, ignoring the she-wolves prostrating themselves trying to gain his attention. I sigh, patting my chosen Beta on the back and letting him grieve. He may be here on my father's orders, but I know he will do his best to save every unmated she-wolf from a cruel fate. It's what his mate would have wanted. The only reason he even came is to prevent my father from giving him a cruel death, having me lose my best friend and support in the pack. I think about how cruel my father is, knowing that Zander lost his mate and unborn pup to an accident that could have been avoided had my father listened to his counsel, and that Zander is not ready to find another love. Even still, that bastard gave my friend two unfair ultimatums.

"I plan to kill him." I state, leaning against my truck as I try to calm the anger that once again rises inside me. My friend looks at me in surprise; his eyes filled with unshed tears.

"Kill who?"

"My father. He needs to go if we are to have a better future." With this, I go into details of my plan, how I did not want Felix to take hold of the title that belongs to me, and how I need to take over as Alpha the moment I reach the lodge. I could not allow my father to rule any longer. Changes need to be made.

"You have my support, and many others too." Zander reassures me, hatred in his eyes. My father is the reason his mate was killed, and I know he wants that bastard dead just as much as I do.

"Do me a favour. Keep an eye out for Karina if you see her. She was forced here, too." I inform my friend before we go our separate ways. He heads to mingle with the other wolves, most likely to find allies, while I head in the direction of the she-wolves, wanting to see who ended up in cages this year.

Walking towards the cages lined and waiting to release their captors, I growl loudly at the males who torment the she-wolves inside, taunting them and explaining the explicit details of how they will be raped and claimed. Idiots, if you ask me. These she-wolves are the ones who refuse to be here. These men will have their hands full if they try anything against these she-wolves. Although killing is prohibited from The Run, fighting and injuring someone is fine as long as it is in self-defence, and I have a feeling many of these males will end up injured the moment they try anything against these she-wolves.

Deciding to walk away, I turn to go back to my truck and wait, maybe catch a nap before we are to enter the forest. But then I see her – a silver wolf curled into a ball resting in her cage. Her fur shimmers with every breath she takes, reminding me of silver glitter used for crafts, mesmerizing me. She is indifferent to her surroundings as if she were anywhere and not at The Run.

A soft smile spreads across my lips. Unlike the she-wolves growling and snarling at any male that draws near, she conserves her energy and strength, not bothering with any male that draws close to her, even as they comment about how boring and weak she probably is. They want someone to break; someone they could slap around. But what they do not see with this silver wolf is the way her tail twitches with each new male that comes near her. The way her ears move towards a certain sound. They could not see the power hidden in her blood, as the way she behaves makes her inconspicuous, but I feel the power in her blood.

Taking a deep breath, I focus on her scent of mint and lavender and chuckle. This silver wolf is of Alpha and Beta blood, with the Alpha blood overpowering her Beta side. She is strong, and she is planning her movements. I have a feeling that this she-wolf will make it out of the forest un-mated and leave a trail of blood and destruction if any male tries to get their hands on her.

While others mingle around me or pass their time taunting the aggressive she-wolves locked away, I silently watch the silver wolf in the cage. I want to get to know her. Learn why she is here and what her view of The Run is. Even help her make it out of the forest unmated so that I can ask her on a date and see what the future holds. I have a feeling that I will find myself flat on my ass the moment we run into each other in the forest, but I am fine with that so long as she gives me a chance. I have never been intrigued by a she-wolf since coming to the event six years ago, when I turned eighteen, and knowing that this Lady Silver has my attention makes me chuckle.

"Hey Caden, I learned from a coordinator that Karina is a nurse this year. She is waiting to help with the injured, so you don't have to worry about her." Zander appears at my side, taking a seat on the ground beside me.

"Good." My answer is short, with my attention still on Lady Silver as the setting sun paints a myriad of colours on her silver fur.

"Something catch your attention?" My best friend chuckles, making my smile grow wider. Pointing towards the first cage in line, I watch my friend's reaction to this rare, furred wolf. He lets out a low whistle before nudging my shoulder with a chuckle.

"A silver wolf to match your golden wolf. Nice." He teases, and I growl warningly at him.

"Yeah, but I plan to get to know her. Take her on a few dates and see where things go." I state, getting a nod of understanding from my friend. Silence settles for a moment before the two of us decide to head back to our cars and wait for The Run to begin, planning what we will do as soon as we enter the forest. We decided that when the time comes, we would go our separate ways into the forest. Keep our pack mates in check and make sure that we make it to the lodge on our last day.

He will find those who are loyal to us and inform them of my plan while I find Lady Silver and get to know her. She won't need my protection, but having an ally may help keep those males at bay. When midnight soon started creeping in, both of us exited my truck and grabbed our bags. Wolves were already shifting, taking in the scent of the female they desired. I chuckle, realizing that Lady Silver had stood up, preparing herself to run. Zander gives me one last hug before heading to a different area.

Ten minutes later, a shift in the air happens, and the silver moon above me begins to turn a sapphire blue. The she wolves that have been growling and snarling nonstop slowly quiet down, moving their focus to the exit of their cage, but still sending warning growls to the males that get too close.

And then it happens.

Then the gunshot rings, and the she-wolves are released.

We all watch in awe as the she wolf in the first cage, the one my eyes have never left, bolts like a bullet. Her silver fur is nothing but a blur, a streak of silver cutting through the blue surroundings. All eyes are on her as she enters the forest at a breakneck speed, long before the others have even made it halfway there.

These males never paid attention to her docile act, and now they lost their chances to gain her scent with the wind blowing in the she-wolves' favour. With a chuckle. I wait for our chance to enter, the ten-minute head start feeling like an eternity. The moment the second gunshot rang out, I watched as the males rushed into the forest, hoping to find the she-wolf they wanted. In no rush, I leisurely walk in. I know I will meet my Lady Silver in no time at all.

Chapter 7 Grace

———

Trees fly past me with every step I take, the different shades of blue blurring together ever so slightly. I take in the scents and sounds of the forest around me, from the sounds of an owl hooting to the right to the sounds of a mouse scurrying in the brush up ahead, my breath coming and going evenly as I maintain a steady gait.

I need to cover as much ground as I can before the men are given a chance to chase after us, to claim us. If I can just find a river or a stream that I can swim until I find a hiding spot and wait out the first few hours out resting and gaining my stamina while the hunt to claim a she-wolf rages on. The forest is quiet, save for a few nocturnal animals running about. No vampires or faeries are seen. Good. I do not want to deal with either of them when The Run has only just begun.

The loud sound of a gunshot rings clear in the quiet night, even if the sound is muffled by the distance. I stop running, realizing that the ten-minute head start is up, and soon the males will be on us, hunting down their prey. With urgency running through my body, I take a deep breath and focus on scenting for water. The scent of pine and maple is the strongest, but something sweet, something clean, enters my nose. Instantly bolting to the left, I make my way towards the clean scent of water and pray to the Moon Goddess to keep me safe for the time being. As I doge more trees, the sounds of wolves crashing through the brush with no regard draw closer, I worry I may not reach a safe hideout before the males get to me.

Suddenly, I find myself falling, realizing I had jumped over a bush and off a four-foot cliff, but the sounds of softly flowing water below me bring a sense of relief, and I shift mid-air into my skin form.

Falling into the cold water, I shiver momentarily from the icy cold plunge before kicking my legs and making my way back to the surface, where I take a deep breath and check to see if my gold earring is still in my cartilage.

Happy to feel the golden hoop, I begin to swim upstream, careful to keep my movements as silent as possible to not be noticed. My best chance of winning the bet and staying mateless for the next seven days is to make my way to the edge of the barrier and walk towards the lodge using the outskirts of the forest.

While swimming, I think back to the days my father had me learn the topography of the Moon Goddess's Forest, wanting me to learn where traps were because no man wants a she-wolf with scars covering her body. I remember the conversation we had, clear as day, after poring over the maps when I turned seventeen, and how my father wanted to prepare me for the next year when I would be participating in The Run for the first time. I remember telling him that learning the topography is useless, as I would not be going due to wanting to find love on my own and not wanting to be raped. Then I remember the bruise his fist left on my face, and the pain radiating from my swollen eye that took a few days to heal. How he expected me to learn the topography within a week or else. The disgust and anger towards the man who sired me as he left me locked away for a week, only able to have a meager amount of food and water. Disgust and anger that to this day remain as strong as ever.

Shaking my head for a moment to rid the thoughts of the past from my mind, I make my way towards a sturdy-looking rock and take a moment to sit, happy that the water still flows over me and carries my scent away. My muscles are starting to grow sore, the cold water finally taking its toll on my body. I will have to find a place to hide soon and warm up if I want to continue my trek without any problems.

With a sigh, I turn to look at the sky, knowing daylight will be coming in a few hours and that many wolves will still be searching for a mate. Once all the weaker she-wolves are taken, the males with some form of power will be hunting for someone like me - a wolf with powerful blood. I won't be able to avoid them if I am exhausted and sleep deprived, and there has to be a shelter somewhere close for me to avoid the wolves searching.

Scanning the trees above me, I carefully look for any clue that a shelter is nearby. A place that can be considered a temporary safe haven for she-wolves who do not want to be mated or a week-long love nest for those who now bear a mate mark. If I can just find one of them – a cave or a treehouse – then there should be some sort of supplies. I am about to give up, to shift and find myself a place I can easily guard and try to recuperate without shelter - but then I see it.

Blowing in the wind, mixed with the long branches of a weeping willow tree, is a white rope ladder that is barely visible if you have no clue what to look for. With a triumphant smirk, I dive back into the river and continue swimming upstream, my body begging me to just rest again. But I keep going. I need to reach safety if I am to get any sleep.

After what feels like an eternity of swimming, I reach the base of the tree, happy to find that the roots and part of the trunk are inside the river, meaning my scent will definitely be hidden if a wolf comes to search for a potential mate. Even though I am exhausted, I swim under the covers of the branches and pause for a moment while I surface once more. Not daring to reach for the rope ladder until I can make sure the area is clear of wolves and I can climb to the safety of the treehouse above; I listen to the quiet night and sniff the air for any scent of a wolf. When I confirm that the coast is clear and that it is safe to leave the water, I grab the rope ladder and climb as quickly and quietly as I can until I find myself inside the small treehouse, one camouflaged and barely noticeable if you aren't paying attention to your surroundings.

Before I can allow my body any rest, I pull the rope ladder inside. I can't have anyone being able to climb in while I sleep, and if I can find the ladder in the night, then it will be easy for those searching for a mate to find it during the day. With the rope ladder secured inside and my body resting against the wall, I take in my little home for the next few hours and realize there is a fresh mattress tucked away from the entrance with a hiking backpack sitting on top.

Grinning like the Cheshire cat, I crawl towards the mattress, careful not to get any water onto it, and pull the backpack off. As soon as I open the bag, I am greeted by a bag of trail mix and a bag of beef jerky that I quickly start munching on, my growling stomach being appeased after being drugged and starved for two days.

Between bites of food, I began taking each item packed by the coordinators of the event out and smiled at my haul. A dry towel is next, something I happily wrap around my wet body to help dry me off quickly, followed by a warm long-sleeve shirt and a pair of pants with a string to tie at the waist. These clothes will keep me warm in the coming days as the chill of the fall air lingers around me, making me shiver.

A pair of runners that thankfully are my size are next to be pulled from the bag, and it takes everything in me not the shout excitedly. These shoes will be perfect for walking through the forest in my skin form, and I need to make sure they are kept safe when I shift. Finally, I find a waterproof flashlight and a metal canteen filled with water that I quickly drink. Later tonight, I will refill it with the clean water from the river below before I continue my seven-day trek to the lodge. After taking stock of what I have, I return the trail mix and remaining jerky to my bag. I'll have to hunt in wolf form if I want to eat anything really filling. Maybe I can find a few faeries and gain some food from them.

Light slowly starts to illuminate the small treehouse, and I look outside the window above the mattress to see the sun beginning to rise, removing the blue hues of the forest and revealing the true colours of the trees. Most she-wolves will keep running now that they can see the forest in the day until their body give out to exhaustion, and that will be their downfall in this barbaric event. The smarter ones will be hiding like me, waiting for nighttime to slink through the trees silently.

With a yawn, I curl up on the soft mattress and close my eyes to sleep. If I leave now, I will be caught instantly, so my best bet is to rest while I have the chance and continue when night has fallen.

Chapter 8 Caden

―――

"Someone help me!" A voice screams out just to my right, causing my left foot to pause mid-step. I want to turn around and rush over to help the woman who is begging, but before I can move, the sounds of clothes being ripped and the groan of a male mid-pleasure follow shortly after her plea. I close my eyes and try to force the rage simmering from within.

A woman, an innocent woman, is being raped, and I am helpless to save her because the mating process has begun, and his mark will be on her soon. I hate this, hate not being able to save this poor she-wolf from her fate, as her heat will soon follow, and the man that just raped her will do it again and again until she is pregnant with his pup. With a silent prayer that this new mate of hers will treat her right, I continue walking, heading towards the river and away from the scene behind me.

It's been an hour since the males were released into the forest, and all around me, the sounds of consensual sex mixed with the nightmarish sounds of rape have sounded. Some girls I have been able to save, scaring the males away with the power of my blood, and giving the she-wolves a hint of where to go if they need a safe path to the lodge. For those with their sweethearts, I leave them be. They already know what they want, so there is no point in my interfering.

My mind has been set on finding Lady Silver as I slowly make my way towards the river, deciding that if I can make it there, I can rest before continuing my search. I am intrigued by her silver fur, a colour only seen every couple of centuries, like my own golden fur. It's rare, and rare means wanted. Any male who saw her curled up indifferently in that cage hours ago will be itching to get their hands on her and make her submit to them. If I can find her, maybe I can talk to her and ask her on a date after we safely reach the Lodge.

Suddenly, I find myself face-first on the ground and a snarling wolf above me with their sharp teeth just millimeters from my neck. Taking a shaky breath, I allow my body to go limp and try my best to be as submissive as possible, or risk whoever it is trapping me from tearing me apart.

"I am not your enemy." My words are quiet, low, and soothing as I try my best to stay calm and not appear as a threat. I am only given a warning growl as the wolf above me presses her paws harder into my back, causing me to wince when I feel her claws poking through the fabric of my shirt and into my skin. I will just have to wait it out and see what happens.

Resigned to my fate, I close my eyes and allow the wolf to decide if I am a threat or not. Crickets fill the night air, and the only other sounds are the occasional growl of the wolf above. I feel myself growing tired from the waiting, wondering if this is where I will be sleeping tonight, as the wolf doesn't seem to want to budge.

Soon, though, my patience seems to be the right move as I feel the paw digging into me slowly becoming gentler until their weight is off my body. Unfortunately for me, the wolf still towers over my body, keeping me trapped. The wolf snarls at the slightest movements I make, and I groan inwardly. There is an itch on my nose I want to scratch, but I have a feeling that if I move, I will find a pair of sharp canines tearing off a piece of flesh from my body.

"Can I sit up, please?" I ask softly after what feels like an hour has passed. I wait for the wolf to answer, their growling subsiding as they shift their weight from paw to paw - most likely debating on if I can be trusted or not.

Another moment of silence passes, and the wolf begins to back away slowly as if waiting for me to try anything and give them a reason to attack. I sigh with relief when the wolf is no longer on top of me and slowly sit up, making sure my movements are visible to the wolf. Now able to sit, I scratch my nose for a moment, happy to be rid of the itch, and come face to face with the wolf that had blindsided me without warning.

Standing across from me, three feet away, is a blonde she-wolf, her fur gently blowing in the wind. I suppress a chuckle when I realize why she is wary of me and keeps me face down on the ground for just over an hour. I had been taken down by a mateless she-wolf who is probably scared out of her mind.

"Don't worry, hun. I have no intentions of claiming a mate." I reassure, slowly sliding my backpack off my back so as not to startle her.

"Would you like a shirt to change into?" I ask, motioning to my bag. The she-wolf eyes me, not sure if she should trust me. To my relief, though, she slowly nods her head and with her blue eyes watching me intently - ready to pounce if I betray her - I pull out a long-sleeve shirt from my bag and hold the black fabric out for her to take. She sends a warning look my way, one that I assume is a 'Don't move or else' warning, before gingerly taking the offered shirt from my hand and trotting behind a large birch tree. I stay where I am, not wanting to feel the sharp teeth of a scared she-wolf ripping through my neck, and wait for her to approach me. I don't have to wait long as a petite blonde-haired, blue-eyed woman comes out, my black shirt falling to her knees and thankfully covering everything from prying eyes.

"Thank you." Her voice surprises me. I expected a quiet, timid voice with her height, but instead I am hit with a power that tells me this she-wolf is of high rank. Maybe a Beta or even an Alpha.

"Don't worry about it." I retort, pushing off the ground and standing, holding my hand out for her to take.

"Caden Wolfrain from Wœlf Haven and future Alpha." Introducing myself, I beam as the she-wolf takes my hand in hers with a firm grip, a small smile on her face as she shakes it.

"Amelia Farefield from Silver Birch. Also, future Alpha." The she-wolf Amelia replies, letting go of my hand to lean against a tree.

"Sorry about tackling you earlier. I thought you were up to something because I caught you staring at my beta, Grace Harvest, at the clearing earlier." Amelia explains with an embarrassed look, running her left hand through her blonde locks.

"I am actually looking for her." She continues, her eyes still watching me with some weariness. I smile sheepishly, trying to figure out who she is talking about.

"What does this Grace Harvest look like?" I ask, running a hand through my hair and yawning. I need to sleep soon, but I have a feeling that if I move now, Amelia will definitely try to rip me apart.

"She is the silver wolf that ran into the forest first. She actually made a bet with my father, and I want to help her. Her winning the bet is the only way for me to be with my boyfriend." She answers, letting out a sad sigh.

"He forced my boyfriend on a scouting mission - most likely intending to kill him - and then forced me to come here in hopes of his only daughter being raped and mated." The blonde continues, pushing a strand of hair out of her face and behind her left ear, where a single gold earring sits. Her weary eyes look exhausted while holding unshed tears, and it takes everything in me not to hug the girl. Unfortunately, her story is like many others here. I lament, looking to the moon and seeing how far it has settled in the night sky.

"My father gave me an ultimatum. Find and bring home a mate or lose my title to my misogynistic, incompetent cousin." I voice without thinking, my own hate simmering in my blood once again. Amelia nods at my statement, most likely knowing that this ultimatum is one that many males most likely have been threatened with into coming to this event because they, too, are unwilling to rape a she-wolf, before she turns and looks in the direction the river is with a knowing smile.

"You want Grace, don't you." She states, catching me off guard.

"What do you mean?" I ask, confused by her words.

"I saw the way you looked at her. You were intrigued, and there was something in your eyes that reminded me of my boyfriend." I blush, taking a moment to think about how I feel about Lady Silver. She intrigued me when I first laid my eyes on her, and to be honest, I wouldn't mind seeing if I can build something with her in the future.

"Yes. I won't force her to mate with me, but I am interested in her and want to ask her out when she makes it out unmatted." I answer honestly, reassuring her that I will not hurt her friend. Her weariness towards me becoming friendly, and I grin. It seems my honesty is the right answer.

"I think she will like that. Most men try to claim her, even within our pack. You'll be the first to actually treat her with respect." I inwardly cheer at Amelia's approval, shocked by how this Alpha wolf trusts me so fast, especially with someone she calls her Beta.

"Anyways, Grace is our best swimmer. She most likely headed towards the river first chance she got." Without hesitation, Amelia takes my hand, and I have just enough time to grab my backpack from the forest floor before this small she-wolf pulls me along behind her. To think someone barely reaching five feet five inches has this much strength. I smile, though, realizing I have gained an ally, and this one is willing to bring me one step closer to getting to know Lady Silver.

Grace Harvest, I can't wait to meet you.

Chapter 9 Grace

———

I watch the horror of the Alpha and his counsel run into the forest chasing the she-wolves of age. Their screams pierce the night. Shivering, I turn to my friend, his fingers clenching into fists as his anger radiates in the air. Carefully, I take his hand in mine and walk away from the blue forest, dragging my friend behind me. He refuses to claim a mate this way, and unfortunately for me, I have one year until I am forced to enter this newfound event. If this is our future, we need to find a way to end it and quickly...

I jerk awake, the screams of a she-wolf piercing my dreams and forcing me awake. She is close, and I can tell a male is chasing her by the way she sobs with fear.

"Stay away from me!" She pleads, her voice pulling at my heart. I want to rush out of this tree house and to her rescue, to bring her away from the male that wants to claim her as his, but instead I curl into a ball and pray that my scent is hidden. I feel like a coward, not running out to help the girl, but if I do, while exhausted, the male will give up on the weaker female for me.

"Come on, baby. Don't you want to feel my hard throbbing cock inside you?" The male taunts, his husky voice filled with lust. Tightly shutting my eyes, I wish that I had not heard that. Wish that I were somewhere then in a tree house listening to a man taunting a woman like she is nothing but a brood mare.

"I said stay away from me!" The she-wolf screams again, but her screams are soon muffled as a loud thud hits the ground and resonates in the air. Silence follows, and I think the she-wolf managed to fight back, until the unmistakable sounds of a man grunting in satisfaction and flesh against flesh break it. The she-wolf has been caught, and the male has claimed a mate. I do my best to block out the sounds of the girl crying as she is raped, but I can't help but think about how painful it must feel to be forced into a mate bond you do not want. Unfortunately for this she-wolf, when her heat comes, she will want his touch. This thought repulses me.

Time passes slowly while the sound of sex is heard loud and clear. No one comes to her aid. Most she-wolves are too focused on hiding and running from a male, and most males are too focused on claiming their own mates. The sounds of sex grow louder as the she-wolf soon gives in, and her cries turn into moans of pleasure. It seems like the male is winning her over. Taking a shaky breath, I send a silent prayer to the Moon Goddess that this she-wolf ends up with this male treating her properly until their climax growls pierce my thoughts and silence follows once more.

"Sorry, hun, but I promise to be a good mate." His voice echoes gently in the silent forest below as his new mate whimpers in agreement. Footsteps along the gravel begin to fade away, and I breathe a sigh of relief. The man left and took his mate with him, reminding me that this tree house is not safe and that I need to go now. I can't risk being caught.

With careful movements, I take the clothes out of my newfound bag and dress as quietly as I can. I did not like feeling exposed and naked on a mattress with only a towel wrapped around me. With a sigh, I place the towel in the bag and strap the pack to my back.

I think about the girl who was just raped, wondering if she will be okay and if someone is looking for her, like I know Amelia will be looking for me. I hope that my best friend has found a place to hide and is making her way to the outer edges of the forest to keep away from the males who are hunting for a strong wolf like her - an Alpha she-wolf with a pack to inherit.

Maybe I should go find her, protect her. We make a great team when fighting, and having someone watch your back while deep in the Moon Goddess' Forest is a blessing I will need. With a sigh, I crawl towards the exit of the tree house, deciding that Amelia knows me best and will search for me upstream of the river. We have an agreement and have settled on a meeting place to head to within three days. If we run into each other along the way, then that will be perfect, but after three days, I will have to move on without her.

Deciding to focus on myself for now, I stick my head out of the hole and listen intently for any sounds of movement, relieved when I realize the coast is clear and I can lower the rope ladder. With a final check, I scurry down and safely onto a tree root, trying to decide which path to take.

The side I am unfortunately on is the opposite riverbank to where I need to be. I will have to swim across if I want to continue going towards the lodge. The only benefit of being on the wrong side of the river is the gravel lining the side, giving me an easy way to conceal my footsteps from any searching wolves.

With a sigh, I carefully jump from root to root until my feet are firmly placed on the ground, careful not to slip on the gravel and make too much noise. With a deep breath, I look up at the sky to see a setting sun through the trees' canopy. Many wolves will be asleep, regaining their energy spent running through last night and all day. Now is my chance to make some ground and find a new place to hide when everyone wakes.

With a small prayer to the Moon Goddess to keep me safe, I start walking upstream, keeping alert for anything lurking in the ever-growing darkness. There is no telling who may be out and about, searching for a mate or a meal. There are still vampire fledglings lurking about that I need to be vigilant for, and I do not intend to become a quick O-negative juice box to a blood sucker.

Chapter 10 Caden

⸻

I watch with worry as the sky begins to brighten and the blue light that bathes the forest slowly fades, realizing just how close daylight is. Amelia and I had found the river about an hour ago, walking along the flow of water upstream in hopes of finding Grace. It seems like this petite blonde did not want to give up until we found her friend. But no matter my protest on needing to find shelter, Amelia keeps going, her resolve stronger than most wolves I have ever met.

"Amelia, we need to find somewhere to sleep before we fall from exhaustion." I state for the umpteenth time, intending to pull the she-wolf to a stop just as her foot slips on the loose gravel, her body falling fast. Luckily, I am close enough to grab her, pulling her body to mine. Her eyes have slightly dark circles under them as she lets out a small yawn. It seems Amelia has hidden her exhaustion from me, even though she reassures me time and time again that she is not tired.

"Just a little longer." She pleads, her words ending in another yawn. I sigh, lifting the woman into my arms and moving forward. I can carry her while we look for Grace, but we need to find someplace safe for the day to rest. Daylight is dangerous for an unclaimed female, and right now Amelia is a hot commodity that most males want.

"If I find a hiding spot before we find Grace, we are going to rest." My voice leaves no room for arguments, and Amelia nods her head against my shoulder in acceptance. She knows her body is at its limit and exhausting herself further is pointless.

"You say Grace is smart, right?" I ask, looking down quickly to see a soft smile on Amelia's face.

"She is the smartest I know." My new friend answers sleepily, pride filling her voice.

"Then she will most likely be sleeping the day away, too." I state, getting a noise of agreement from the exhausted she-wolf in my arms.

"We have plenty of time to catch up to her, so don't worry, we will find her." I reassure the now yawning Alpha wolf in my arms. I chuckle and tuck her head under my chin, trying my best to shield her from the wind.

"Caden, when we leave this place, will you form a treaty with me and my pack?" Her voice is quiet, sleep slowly taking its hold on her. I smile, holding back another chuckle as I think about Karina and how similar the blonde in my arms is to her.

"Yes. I was thinking of asking you the same thing." It seems my answer surprises her as she shifts in my arms to look at me, nearly making me drop her.

"Really?" She asks in disbelief. I nod, keeping my eyes open for any signs of silver fur.

"Yes. You are a good Alpha, and I want allies like you." I answer honestly, looking down at her for a moment before returning my gaze to the forest around the river, continuing my search.

"I'm glad I met you then." She yawns out, settling back into my arms. Silence follows, and I listen as Amelia dozes off against me, and do my best to stay quiet while I trek on ahead. Luckily, I spy the signs of a cave nearby and head just right of the river, where I find the entrance to the hiding spot just a few feet into the tree line. Relieved to find a place so soon to spend the day, I rush inside to find a thankfully unused mattress and gently place Amelia on top, drop my own bag at the foot of the bed, and run out to mark the entrance the best way I know how.

"Hey man, you bag yourself a mate?" Someone calls out, making me jump. Suppressing a growl of annoyance, I turn just in time to watch four males emerging from a couple of bushes to my right and decide that I have to interact with them to keep Amelia and me safe.

"Yep, an Alpha Female. Guess I'll be running a pack now." I answer, leaning against the entrance behind me and blocking them from scenting out Amelia. The males look at one another with envy before turning to face me once more.

"Damn man, the lap of luxury is yours after The Run ends. You got lucky." A black-haired wolf with tanned skin congratulates me, his eyes looking towards the cave entrance behind me, his eyes filled with jealousy.

"He's right. Anyways, have fun with the she-wolf and wish us luck in finding our own." The one to call out to me, a brunet wolf with a scar along his cheek, agrees with the black-haired wolf, giving me a smirk. With a wave, the four leave, their hunt for a mate still ongoing. I exhale a breath I did not know I was holding, relieved that those men did not try and fight me for Amelia.

Now alone, I mark the entrance of the cave with my scent before heading inside. Sleep is calling me, but I know these little hiding spots are filled with treasures for participants to use. Deciding to see if there is anything useful for Amelia inside the cave, I look around and quickly spot a backpack in the corner. I walk towards it, lifting it up and testing its weight. Surprised by how decently heavy it is, I set it down beside the bed and sigh. I am happy to see that there is something here that will be useful for my new friend, but I will leave it up to Amelia to go through it when we wake up, since everything in there will be hers.

For now, we both need sleep if we want to continue searching for her Beta. With a yawn, I join Amelia on the mattress and quickly fall asleep. My scent will be on her when we wake, and hopefully, this will keep her safe as we travel together.

Chapter 11 Grace

———

The feeling of being watched washes over me, creating goosebumps along my arms. My steps pause briefly as I slowly move away from the water and off the gravel lining the river shores. I have a feeling someone – or something – is stalking me like prey, and if I need to protect myself, I would rather do it on solid ground and not on gravel slick from the river water.

Something inside me screams that this thing is not a wolf, leaving only two options – Fae or Vampire. I prefer it if it were the Fae, as they are easier to deal with. If it is a Vampire, then that means a fledgling has found me.

I continue forward, keeping my senses alert for any movements that will come my way and preparing myself for anything. If it's a Fae, I will have to stop moving and talk to them, reassure them I am not a threat, and show them the token on my ear. If it is a vampire, I will have to be ready to fight to the death.

The forest slowly quiets, the sounds of nightlife fading away until an eerie silence is left. Taking a deep breath, I close my eyes and try to pinpoint where the threat is coming from, opening my senses to the forest around me and taking a deep breath. The feeling of being watched has moved from behind me to in front of me, and I dodge backwards just in time for a blurry figure to come crashing by, smashing into the large oak tree.

Dropping my backpack, I eye the figure sprawled out on their back at the base of the tree, waiting to see what will happen.

Turns out I don't have to wait long as they spring to their feet, turning to face me with blood red eyes and fangs dripping with Vampire venom. I have come face-to-face with one of the ten fledglings. Its slim body and long hair lead me to believe this fledgling used to be a beautiful female, but now is nothing but a bloodthirsty monster. The fledgling lets out a loud, blood-curdling scream before rushing me, swiping its claw-like hands in my direction, trying to land a blow.

I carefully dodge, doing my best to stay on solid ground and lead the fledgling away from the river. I need to find a sharp branch to spear them with and soon, or worse, be killed and drained of blood by this thing.

With a split-second decision, I turn my back on the fledgling and rush towards a fallen tree I spotted just after leaving the tree house, hearing the fledgling thrashing around the bushes behind me, hunting me down. I will be a juice box for them soon if I can't kill them.

A snap to my right has me veering a hard left as the fledgling crashes into the spot I just vacated. Without a second thought, I continue sprinting towards the direction I remember the fallen tree being, turning to look back for a second to see the fledgling stand, look around, and seem confused with what appears to be a branch stuck in its abdomen. Good. The branch will slow it down.

Returning my gaze to the forest around me, I focus on the task at hand, pushing myself forward until finally I emerge from the bushes directly in front of my target and get to work ripping off a sturdy branch from the fallen birch tree while listening to the forest. The last thing I need is the fledgling attacking me while I am busy. With a loud crack, the branch I need comes off, the tip of it perfectly sharp, ready to shish kabob the fledgling. I will only have one chance to plunge this into the heart of my pursuer or pray that some help arrives to kill it with me.

I don't have to wait too long for the fledgling to track me down, as the sounds of it thrashing through the brush can be heard growing closer, its shrieking loud and clear tells me it is coming fast. Crouching with my back against the fallen tree, I position the branch and wait, making sure to keep my breathing even and calm my pounding heart. I think right now I would rather be dealing with a horny male than a deadly fledgling out of control.

Finally, the thing emerges, its body rushing towards me with new twigs stuck inside its skin, slowing it down. I count each step it takes, grinning when the perfect time comes, and I thrust the branch up into its chest directly where its dead heart should be. The fledgling releases a feral cry, forcing me to release the branch and cover my ears as the piercing sound of its voice causes me to wince in pain. I keep watching it, waiting to see if I will have to dodge any new attacks, but let out a relieved sigh when the skin around the branch begins to crack.

The cracks continue to grow, getting bigger and bigger as microfractures spread out from it like concrete being hit with a sledgehammer until finally, pieces of the fledgling splinter off. The fledgling falls to its knees in front of me, reaching for my body in futility until it collapses, dead. When sunlight comes, its body will burn into nothing but dust and ash.

Relieved I survived a fledgling, I lean back on the fallen tree behind me to catch my breath. If I make it out of this event alive, I will be demanding an award from the Ancient Eli for exterminating his mistake.

After calming my frantic heart and catching my breath, I start the trek back to where I dumped my bag, happy to see that no one came by and took it the moment I spot my backpack still in the place I left it. Picking up the backpack and throwing it onto my shoulders, I check my surroundings before setting off upriver once more. I have to be careful because if any wolves are around, they most likely have heard the commotion caused by the fledgling and will be on their way towards me right now. I have to get as far away as possible from here and quickly find some place to hide out in just in case.

My mind wanders to what reward I may receive from Eli. Being an Ancient, he most likely has collected some good items over the years. Maybe I will ask for a few weapons or an expensive paint set. Maybe even a house of my own. Anything would be good, really. I chuckle, thinking about how a house of my own would be great. I can use it as a rental if it is in the human cities and gain some form of income away from what the Alpha pays me.

Suddenly, strong arms grab me from behind, and I find myself pressed against a sturdy tree; a well-toned body pressed into my back with signs of an erection grinding into my ass. I had forgotten to keep my senses alert, and it seems I had made a mistake as the scent of a male fills my nose, reminding me that this forest is a dangerous place for an unmated she-wolf.

"Hello, my dear prize."

Chapter 12 Caden

Blood drips down my face as a man laughs. His brown hair is the only feature I can make out while the painful wails of a she-wolf ring through the air. It is hopeless.

The Run has become a popular event amongst the men, but the King wants one she-wolf as his, and he has captured her.

Tears stream down my face as the hope I had for our future vanishes with each grunting noise the King makes in claiming the woman I love as his mate...

The sounds of night animals startle me from my sleep, waking me from the nightmare that felt all too real. Nightmares that always left me wondering if they were just my imagination or of a past life.

Sighing, I go to sit up only to notice a warm body snuggled into me, trapping me where I lie. Amelia is wrapped around me, her blonde hair splayed out behind her as she sleeps without any worry. With another sigh, I slowly pry the she-wolf's grip from around my body and climb off the mattress as soon as I am free to stretch.

My mind wanders to the dreams that come and go, dreams of a lady dressed in ball gowns and a man wearing a long coat and breeches tucked into tall leather boots. They seem all too familiar. Like I knew them personally. I can still hear that woman's all too haunting screams as she is raped in my dreams. Hear the grunting of someone taking her without fail. Were these dreams of the past, or just my mind running wild while I participate in The Run?

An owl hooting outside the cave breaks me from my thoughts and reminds me that Amelia and I will have to leave the cave soon. For now, checking outside and focusing on the task of finding Lady Silver should be my priority.

Walking out of the cave, I lean against the entrance and scan my surroundings, keeping my senses alert for any signs of movement before turning my gaze to the twilight sky. It looks as if the sun has just set, meaning now will be a good time to continue on foot. Amelia and I will be safe from the wolves looking for a mate, as many will be asleep or already deeper into the Goddess's forest. Making my way back inside, I spot Amelia now curled into a ball in the center of the mattress, the sight of her innocence bringing a chuckle to my lips as I think about how vulnerable this she-wolf is. She is lucky I am the one to have run into her and not some other wolf, as she would have been claimed by now with how heavy a sleeper she is.

"Amelia, it's time to wake up." I call out, walking closer to the mattress and bending down to gently shake her shoulder. She groans in response, batting away my hand. Rolling my eyes, I shake her slightly harder, repeating my words, only to be met with a low warning growl.

"Amelia, we need to find Grace." I growl out, allowing the power in my blood to merge with my words. She bolts awake, her sleep-filled eyes staring at me in confusion and fear for a moment before realizing it is just her and me in the cave.

"Goddess Caden, you scared me." She huffs out, her hand on her chest, most likely trying to calm her frantic heart. I smile apologetically, standing straight and grabbing my backpack. I know why my command scared her, but I am not ready to explain anything just yet.

"We need to get going." I state, leaving no room for her to protest.

"It's nighttime, and it is the best time to keep searching for your beta." I continue, leaning against the cave wall and allowing the she-wolf to stand and stretch before she, too, grabs the newly obtained backpack I left for her. I can see her curiosity as she gives me a look before instantly rummaging through the bag. Slightly impatient, I wait for her to look into her new supplies and roll my eyes when Amelia lets out a little yip of excitement and pulls out a pair of sneakers, quickly slipping her feet into them.

"We can walk faster now!" She exclaims, zipping the backpack shut and throwing it over her shoulders. I silently agree that her acquiring shoes is a good thing. It means we can cover more ground and not worry about her feet being injured while in the forest.

With the two of us now ready, we make our way out of the cave and back to the river. It's our best chance at finding Amelia's Beta and my best chance at meeting her. We follow up the stream of the river, our conversation low so that we do not attract attention. The last thing we need is a Vampire fledgling or a male wolf coming out to attack us.

There are signs of life along the river, and Amelia and I are careful to investigate if Grace's scent lingers around or not. Sadly, no scent of mint and lavender can be found other than from the plants themselves, and I sigh, feeling defeated at not being able to find the she-wolf I long to meet.

"Do you think we will find her tonight?" Amelia asks as we find a fallen tree to sit on, taking a break from walking to sip on the water in the canteen and devour a bag of trail mix from Amelia's bag.

"I am not sure." I answer honestly, taking a look at the sky and seeing the blue moon shining down on us. At least three hours have passed since we woke up and began walking. I am shocked we have yet to come across anyone. Suddenly, a group of wolves comes crashing through the bushes, and I force Amelia to stand behind me, only to notice Zander among the four wolves, the three others being Mike, Caleb, and Cody from my pack. I am about to greet them, but I notice their fur standing straight and the scent of blood emanating from Cody and Mike. Something attacked them. I don't have to wait too long to see what attacked my friends when two fledglings come running out after the four, my blood boiling at seeing my packmates in danger.

"Amelia, go hide. I have to help them." I order through clenched teeth, handing my bag to the blonde.

"Why can't we just run away?" She asks, her fear for the newborn Vampires evident in her voice. No one wants to fight a strong, fast, and starving fledgling.

"These four are pack mates of mine. One of them is my future Beta." With that, I kick off my shoes and shift into my golden wolf, the sounds of my clothes shredding as my paws dig into the forest floor below me.

[Zander, with me. Cody, Mike, and Caleb take the female, and we will take the male.] I order through the link, rushing to the left as Zander changes direction quickly and flanks my right side. Caleb, his twin Cody, and Mike are happy to have a helping hand spin on their hind paws and rush to attack the female.

[What's the plan?] Cody asks, dodging a swipe of claws as I dodge a kick from the male before me.

[Taking turns to attack and retreat. We need to wear it down before we can kill them.] I explain, getting a resounding "Yes Alpha" from my four friends through our link. I look to Zander and nod, taking the lead to rush the male, distracting it as Zander takes this chance to bite the side of the Vampire. When the fledgling turns to attack Zander, I rush and claw at its shoulder, backing away just in time to dodge its sharp claw-like hands. I notice the other three doing a similar technique, proud of my Warriors before returning to help Zander take down the male.

The fight continues, and without realizing it, I find myself closer to the river. When dodging the next attack from the fledgling, my paws slip in the mud, giving the Vampire an open shot at attacking. I brace myself for the pain of jagged, sharp claws ripping through my fur and flesh, seeing the look of panic in Zander's eyes as he is too far to help me.

Suddenly, a flash of blonde fur leaps over the vampire, the wolf's claws landing a blow to their head and knocking the Vampire down, giving me a chance to climb to my feet and attack, my jaw biting down on the Vampire's leg and ripping it off at the knee. I rush away, just barely missing being hit by their claws, and look to see Amelia rushing to attack, Zander already taking this chance to rip off the arm of the fledgling, while the she-wolf grabs the medium-length hair of the vampire and pulls. I rush forward, grabbing the only remaining arm before the fledgling could claw at my friend, and begin pulling in the opposite direction. With a sickening sound of flesh tearing, Amelia decapitates the Vampire, and I am left standing in awe at my new friend's bravery.

[No one touch her!] I order through the link as Cody, Caleb, and Mike join us, their eyes looking at the female with curiosity.

[Why, you already claim her Alpha?] Caleb asks, and I growl at him.

[She has someone already; her father sent him away in hopes of him dying.] I answer, seeing the guilt in Caleb's eyes as he looks to Zander, most likely thinking about how our friend lost his mate and unborn pup. With that, Amelia nudges me, then points towards the trees before trotting away.

[She wants us to follow her.] I interpret to the others before trotting after the blonde, seeing her enter a cave not too far away from where we once sat on the fallen tree. It seems Amelia has a good understanding of the forest.

With a sigh of relief, I follow her inside and quickly shift, ignoring Amelia as she finishes putting on her clothes. Digging through my bag, I pull out a pair of sweatpants and a t-shirt, dressing quickly. Zander is the first to enter the cave, a couple of minutes later, followed by Mike and the twins, the four in their human forms dressed in sweat pants and t-shirts as well, with their bags slung over their shoulders. One of them must have gone back to grab their backpacks before joining Amelia and me in the cave.

"Sup, Caden's friends." Amelia greets, already munching on her beef jerky.

"Uh, hi." Zander replies confused, looking to me with a puzzled look.

"I am just helping her find her friend Grace." I state, accepting the piece of jerky Amelia holds out to me and taking a bite. That fight took a lot out of me, but we still have plenty of nighttime to keep going.

"Ah, the Golden boy continues to save she-wolves." Mike chuckles out, plopping himself on the floor before taking out his canteen and drinking heartily from it. I roll my eyes, leaning against the wall and taking a deep breath.

"Thanks for the help, Caden. We got ambushed by those two fledglings after a feral cry was heard by another one. I have a feeling three are dead now." Cody sighs out, sliding down the cave wall to sit, his eyes on Amelia.

"Thank you too, blondie. You got some big balls taking on a fledgling." Amelia chuckles at Mikes praise, chucking a piece of jerky to the brunette before continuing to devour the bag in her lap.

"You should really save those." I suggest, getting an eye roll in return.

"The bag over there has ten packs. Let me enjoy mine." She mumbles through a mouthful, causing the others in the cave to chuckle.

"Did you notice the wolf who killed the other Vampire?" Amelia asks, turning her attention away from me to my friends.

"A girl with silver hair. But that was two hours ago." Cody answered absentmindedly, looking towards the bag Amelia pointed at before getting up and taking out a bag of jerky. He promptly starts handing out a bag to each of us, leaving five in the bag in case any she-wolf comes across this cave and needs some food. I smile at his consideration before grabbing one more bag and handing it to Amelia. She already shared the bag she is munching on with us; the least I can do is make sure we have another when we find Grace.

"You said a girl with silver hair. That must be Grace." Amelia jumps up from her spot, stuffing the beef jerky in her backpack before turning to me. I smile, already knowing her intention before turning to my pack mates, who look on with amused smiles.

"If you come across that she-wolf again, her name is Grace. Tell her Amelia is looking for her and is safe and unmated." I state to my friends as Amelia looks at me impatiently.

"All of you stay safe and alive." I add, walking over to Zander and hug him, proud that my friend found pack mates we can trust.

"You two stay safe too." Caleb replies back, a smile on his face.

"And remember Alpha, we've got your back when The Run ends. Just give us a link when you need us." Nodding, I accept his words before Amelia and I head out again. Knowing Grace has a two-hour head start on us after dealing with a fledgling, I have a feeling Amelia is just filled with worry and wants to see her Beta and best friend as soon as possible.

Chapter 13 Grace

The scent of the male behind me reminds me of the situation I am in, with my body stuck between his lean body and the tree, I am helplessly trapped unless I can find a way to get clear. I curse myself for not paying attention and allowing my mind to wander. If I had kept a clear head, I would not be where I am now. His scent is rich with power as he growls possessively towards me. My guess is this wolf is a Beta, maybe an Alpha wolf still coming into his power.

"You smell delicious, little girl." He chuckles, his lips pressing against the crook of my neck as he takes in my scent. I shiver with disgust, waiting for the right moment to throw him off me, but I keep calm. If I attack now, I will find myself stripped of my clothes and at his mercy in no time. Hands begin to roam my body, staring from my thighs, slowly groping and gliding along my curves, and ending at my breasts. His fingers firmly grope my breasts, grinding his erect cock into my ass and moaning with satisfaction. I take a deep breath, reminding myself not to panic as lust from the male permeates the air.

"I bet you like this baby. All my attention on your body?" His voice is a husky whisper as he places kisses along my neck, teeth grazing a spot I have a feeling he wants to mark.

"I bet you are just waiting to be fucked, to be filled with my cock and made mine." He chuckles, squeezing my breasts one more time before his left hand descends from my breast and slowly down my abdomen, going lower until I feel him between my legs, rubbing small circles through the pants I am wearing. I shudder, thankful for the small barrier of fabric. If he were to dip his hands under my waistband, he would be able to slip a finger inside me.

"Get horny for me, gorgeous, and I will make you mine." His tongue flicks across my skin, making me shiver again. Goddess knows I want to bathe in bleach right now. To scrub away this scum's touch and his scent off my body.

With a squeal of surprise, my body is turned around, and the wolf before me smashes his lips to mine, kissing me with greedy passion. My eyes are wide, shocked by the audacity of this male, while I force myself not to turn my nails into claws and rip out his heart. His right hand continues to grope my breast, while the other moves to grab my ass, pressing my body closer to his as I feel his erection twitch through the thin fabric of our clothes. This gives me an idea as I slowly kiss the wolf back. If I want to get free, I need to play along.

My left hand is pressed against his chest, giving me a bit of space between our bodies, while my right hand trails down his body towards his erection, gently teasing him through the fabric of his shorts. He pulls away with a shudder, resting his head on my shoulder as he lets out a moan.

"Mmm, yes, baby, grab my cock." He groans out and I smirk, letting this disgusting excuse of a wolf lead my right hand right into the shorts he his wearing and directly onto his hard cock. Checkmate.

"You know, you should be very careful of which she-wolf you trap." I chuckle out quietly, my fingers slowly curling around the base of his penis as I stroke it slightly, feeling him shudder from pleasure.

"Why's that baby?" He questions, his nose grazing my neck.

"Because you might end up unable to have children." With my words, I clench my fingers tightly into his skin, feeling his cock go limp as he lets out an ear-piercing scream. I wince, making sure my hold on him tightens while slowly tugging, hearing a squelching noise and feeling the warmth of blood gush between my fingers.

"P-please. L-let me go!" He whimpers, tears streaming down his face. I release his now mangled appendage, watching as the wolf who was ready to rape me just minutes earlier crumbles to the ground. With a grin, I grab his filthy brown hair and throw his face into the tree he had pinned me on, slamming his face into the rough bark over and over again until his skin is left a bloody mess.

"Remember me and this beating next time you try to rape someone." I growl out, enjoying the fear in his eyes before he passes out from the pain. Letting go of the wolf, I back away for a moment and shudder. I need to leave, as others will soon come to see what the scream was, and I do not want to be here when even more males show up.

Taking one last look at the unconscious male, I turn around and continue walking. After I feel like I am a safe distance, I carefully make my way towards the river and strip, throwing my clothes into my bag and quickly rinsing off the blood and scent of that disgusting male. The cool water refreshes me, and with reluctance, I return to my bag on the shore and use the towel to dry off before throwing my clothes back on. I need to continue walking now that I am clean. Unfortunately for me, morning will be coming fast, and I have ground to cover before the sun rises.

Chapter 14 Caden

The cry of a male echoing through the quiet night causes my steps to falter and my skin to crawl. I have never heard such a blood-curdling scream before, and the only thing I can think of is that this male most likely messed with the wrong she-wolf. Amelia chuckles, her eyes holding a hint of bloodlust inside their blue depth.

"Seems like some egotistical male found a she-wolf and lost whatever fight they were having." She states, continuing forward as if the scream meant nothing to her. I take a shuddering breath, praying that whoever harmed the male won't harm me if they see Amelia and me traveling together as we continue trekking through the forest.

We come to the riverside once more, deciding to refill our canteens with the fresh water before we continue searching for Grace. The sounds of animals have died down, leaving the area silent with only the sound of the river bubbling beside us. With an agreement for our safety, talking is kept to a minimum, with the two of us not wanting to attract any attention in case wolves come to investigate that scream. Being silent gives us a chance to get away unnoticed.

"I have a feeling we are getting closer to where that scream came from." I point out while the sounds of wildlife slowly decrease to nothing. Amelia nods in response, shifting closer to my side while her eyes scan our surroundings.

"I agree. Which means there is another she-wolf in the area." She mumbles out. Looking at her from the corner of my eye, I see a hint of sadness in her face. I worry for her, even if we have only known each other for a short time. She reminds me of my sister.

"Are you okay, Amelia?" I ask, taking hold of her hand and pulling her to a stop. She looks away, hiding her face from me, but I notice the tears slipping past her eyes and rolling down her cheeks. Gently, I wipe them away and pull her in for a hug, one I feel like she desperately needs. Within a few short hours, she was ripped away from her boyfriend because of her father and sent to The Run, with his hopes of her being raped and claimed by a man he approves of, being her father's priority. Not only that, but she was separated by the only person she can trust.

"I'm scared." She whimpers out, her hands fisting in my shirt as she trembles in my arms. Pain and fear radiate off of her, and I now understand that she has been putting up a brave front. This poor girl. To go through so much so young makes me wonder what kind of life she and Grace live in Silver Birch.

"I just want to go home to my Bryden." She states with a quiver in her voice, her sadness breaking my heart. We stand in silence as I let Amelia cry into my chest. It must be hard, being separated from the person she loves, not knowing if he will live or die while she is trapped here at The Run. Unable to decide her own fate. I allow her to lean on me while I keep my senses alert, hoping that no wolf comes our way so that Amelia can compose herself. After a few minutes, her tears slow, and her shaky breathing begins to even out. With a relieved smile, I pull away from her and wipe away her tears.

"Better?" I ask, getting a small nod from her as she sniffles.

"Good, let's get moving and find Grace. I want to help her win this bet between your father and her." I add cheerfully, poking her nose and getting a giggle out of Amelia.

"Thanks, Caden." She whispers, smiling brightly at me.

"For what?" Confused, I look at her, trying to see what Amelia is thinking.

"For not taking advantage of me and for being a friend." She answers. I smile, pulling her in for another hug and reassuring Amelia that as soon as we get done with The Run, I will form an alliance treaty with her before we continue our journey of finding Grace. The forest is still so quiet, but I keep my senses alert just in case something or someone pops out of the bushes.

"Do you think the Fae are around here?" Amelia asks, and I shake my head.

"No. They prefer the middle of the forest. It's easier to trap wolves there with them." I answer quietly. Amelia nods before going back to sniffing the air every couple of steps. I decide that I will keep a lookout while she focuses her energy on sniffing out Grace. She knows Grace's scent by heart and is our best chance at finding her Beta lies with Amelia. Our walk brings us closer to a willow tree just a couple of feet away, one that has a rope ladder swinging with the branches in the breeze.

"I can smell her!" Amelia exclaims in delight, her eyes widening as she makes a beeline for the willow tree. I chase after her, worried that the noise will attract the males in the area. As soon as I reach the base of the tree, mint and lavender fill my nose, and I sigh. She smells delicious.

"She's not here, but it looks like she spent the night. We might have missed her by an hour, maybe two." Amelia exclaims loudly, pulling me from my thoughts. I think back to what my pack mates told me and nod, the time frame matching up. If the fledgling they saw Grace fighting attacked her around here, then we should soon see signs of a fight.

"Do you know which direction she might have headed?" I ask, getting a grin as a response.

"She is making her way to the outer borders. If we keep walking upriver, we might be able to spot her soon." After some thinking, Amelia answers.

"Then let's keep walking." I happily state, letting Amelia lead the way. Making sure to keep her close to me in case of any danger, Amelia happily leads our trek upriver once again, her blue eyes shining with excitement at the possibility of finding Grace. She has her nose in the air once again scenting for Grace, but even I can smell the mint and lavender growing stronger with each step we take.

The farther from the willow tree we go, the more I notice the signs of battle, pointing out a few broken branches and the scent of a vampire nearby, only for Amelia to confirm that Grace did, in fact, fight a fledgling. I can tell that with each claw mark we see on a tree, Amelia grows increasingly worried, most likely wondering about Grace and her fight with a Vampire fledgling.

"Do you think she got injured?" She asks, her voice quiet as we step over a log. I go to answer her, only to spot the unmoving body over her shoulder, not to far from where we stand, and I chuckle, looking at Amelia and giving her a reassuring smile.

"I think she is fine and that she won the fight." I state, hoping to reassure her while pointing to the dead fledgling. She smiles, looking at the body and letting out a sigh of relief as we turn away from the body and continue following the trail of destruction caused by the fight between Grace and the Fledgling.

"Grace should have been an Alpha." After some silence, Amelia lets out this small statement, making me think about the wolf in the cage and how she was indifferent to the wolves' leering at her.

"She is too strong to stay as a Beta." She continues, her voice low and almost inaudible, but the feeling of pride coming from Amelia is one I cannot miss. If Grace is so strong that she can take on a fledgling and win, then I wonder just how much stronger she will become in the future with continuous training.

A comfortable silence falls between us once more as we follow Grace's scent, the path leading us away from the river and through the forest, where more remnants of fighting can be seen. I am shocked by the sheer destructive power of a fledgling and excited to meet the woman who killed one.

But our trek through the trees ended, and we emerged near the side of the river once more after the detour the scent trail took us through, and I wonder just what kind of path Grace took. It seems both these she-wolves know the forest well, even if this is their first time entering The Run.

Walking close to the river, my nose scrunches up in disgust as the iron tang scent of blood reaches my nose, making me look around for the source and putting Amelia behind me as we cautiously walk forward. The forest is silent in the dead of night, with only a few nocturnal creatures making the barest of sounds, and I reach out my senses to see if anyone else is around. Sadly, I do not sense anything other than a wolf a few feet away, lying beside a tree.

"Stay behind me, Amelia, and let's see who is lying there." I whisper out, the blonde nodding her head in understanding. We stay close to the treeline, allowing the shadows created by the moonlight to hide our bodies as we creep closer to the wolf. The scent of blood grows stronger the closer we get, and as soon as we get close enough for a better look, I notice why the wolf hasn't moved.

His face is torn, and I am unable to identify who this wolf is. Some scrapes are already in the process of healing thanks to being a werewolf, but other than that, I have no other idea why he would be unconscious.

"He is bleeding." Amelia states, and I sigh.

"Yeah, I see. His face should be healed soon." I shrug, wondering if I should do anything to help this wolf.

"No, I mean in his pants." My eyes dart to the spot Amelia is pointing to, and I shudder, my hand instantly moving to subconsciously protect my own cock, feeling sympathy for the man. To think someone would mutilate his manhood like that to the point of being unable to create pups at most for a year.

"Who would do something like that to a man?" I question quietly, backing away a few steps.

"Grace. I can guarantee he was trying to rape her." Amelia deadpans, her eyes cold as a murderous aura surrounds the she-wolf. All the sympathy I had is now gone; only disgust is left. I sniff the air, searching past the blood to find the mint and lavender underneath. Grace was here, and luckily, she left unmated and with a warning to all males. I can't help but feel pride for a wolf I have never met.

"Remind me never to piss her off." I mumble out with slight fear, taking Amelia's hand and leading the woman away. I have a feeling that if we stay in this spot any longer, she might kill this wolf for harming her friend, and I can't allow that, as much as I want to. There are cameras in the forest, and if she were to kill, she would be captured and executed as soon as The Run ends. As soon as we are far enough away and the smell of blood no longer lingers in the air, I release Amelia's hand and continue walking beside her.

We continue walking along the river, the water soothing my mind, making me yawn, my tired body reminding me that we have been walking for hours searching for Grace. Morning will be here any moment, meaning we will need to find a cave or treehouse as soon as possible to sleep. Wolves will be out looking for a mate as soon as the sun is up, and we are becoming too exhausted to fight back if any stumble upon us.

"Amelia, we need to find shelter." I grab her wrist, pulling Amelia to a stop beside me. She growls, trying to pull away, but stopping to yawn.

"She is close, Caden, I can feel her." Amelia protests, her eyes looking into mine. I sigh, seeing the unshed tears she holds back, and pull her in for a hug.

"I know Amelia. But it will be morning soon, and you need to sleep and avoid any males leaving their hideaways to look for a mate." I reason with her, pulling her towards the tree line once more. If I am not mistaken, there is a cave somewhere near us, and we will need to get to it quickly.

"Caden, let go." Amelia pulls at my hand, trying to free herself from my grasp, but she is tired, I can hear it in her voice.

"I will when we get to the cave." I retort with. She growls, her fingers shifting until I wince and end up letting go of her to see three claw marks along my wrist. She had transformed her nails into claws and clawed me.

Growling in frustration, I turn to scold her for hurting me, only to see a look of shock in her eyes as she looks behind me. Before I can turn around, I hear the snapping of a twig and my body being tackled to the ground, a snarling wolf above me with their fangs around the back of my neck. Mint and lavender fill my nose, and I relax under the weight of this snarling wolf as soon as I realize who has tackled me.

We have finally found Grace.

Chapter 15 Grace

———

I groan, leaning against an oak tree as I try to think of where the hidden cave may be. An hour has already passed since I mutilated that male who tried to rape me, and I barely made it three kilometers away until the scent of dawn started blowing on the wind.

Fighting that fledgling took up too much of my time, time that I could have used to cover much-needed ground. Morning will be here soon, and I will need to find a place to sleep for a few hours before I continue to race towards the lodge.

But worry gnaws at me.

I haven't seen Amelia after her cage was carried away before the event started. I wonder if she, too, has found a place to hide and stay safe to avoid the males.

Looking up at the still full moon in the sky, I question whether or not I should go and find her, to bring her along with me to the lodge and keep both of us unmated. This would definitely anger her father to have both me winning the bet and his only child unmated and not bringing home a male to take over the pack from him.

I think back to Amelia and me studying the map a week before The Run began, how we planned to follow the river and meet up eventually if we were separated at a cave within three days. Today is already the second day of The Run, with daylight breaking, and we have until midnight tomorrow for the two of us to meet up. I curse, taking in my surroundings, and realize that the cave we had decided to meet up at is about a ten-minute walk back in the direction I just came from. Maybe I should rest there for the day and see if Amelia will show by tomorrow night. If not, I will have to go on without my best friend and hope she makes it to the lodge unmated.

I sigh, pushing off the rock and making my way back towards the cave, my body sore and worn out already. Between the fledgling and that perverted male wolf, I need a good night's rest. Thankfully, it is still dark out, meaning it is still safe for me to continue traveling and avoid the few wolves that hunt for a mate in the night. I am lucky that the majority of those participating in The Run prefer to travel the forest during the day when light helps them to see the many traps laid about. Sunlight also helps them to avoid the Fae, since most Fae prefer to play tricks under the cover of night.

Now add a few Vampire fledglings to the mix, and traveling in the day is much safer for any wolf, preferably the weak she-wolves and males, but it is dangerous for me. I would rather face another fledgling than another wolf desperate to claim a female as their own again.

Sticking to the shadows of the trees, I retrace my steps towards the cave, having to walk away from the river and turn left to make it to my next hiding spot after walking back about five kilometers. I can see the sky above me brightening with the sun creeping up. Soon, the wolves participating in this event will be waking up either to hunt prey and feed their new mate or to hunt a she-wolf to mate. I need to make it inside and mask my scent quickly before any of them tracks me down.

Keeping my senses alert, already having learned my lesson, I pad through the forest quietly until the cave entrance comes into view, filling me with relief. My safety lies just a few feet away, and I rush the rest of the journey, making it to the entrance just in time to watch the sky slowly become shades of pinks, purples, and reds. I can already imagine the soft mattress that I cannot wait to sleep in as I am about to duck under the short entrance when the wind brushes past me, making my steps freeze as an all too familiar scent reaches my nose – Amelia's scent.

I am ecstatic to know she is so close to me, that she made it to our rendezvous location before I am forced to let her fend for herself, ready to wait for her inside the cave, and surprise my friend. That is, until another gust of wind brings her scent close to me, this time stronger and mixed with another's scent – a male's scent.

I growl, feeling my happiness turn into fear and anger for my friend. Without a second thought, I rush into the cave and throw my bag into the far corner, taking off my clothes before running out of the cave once more, shifting mid-step into my silver wolf. I wince from the slight pain the shift causes, but push forward and keep downwind while the scent of decaying leaves in the fall air fills my nose, making me want to sneeze, but I remain silent, reminding myself that Amelia may be in danger right now.

I have to get to her before the sun rises, take out the male, and bring Amelia to safety.

I promised Bryden that if Amelia and I met up during The Run, I would protect her and keep her safe for him long before the bet between the Alpha and me was made. The scent of the male - fresh forest on a winter's day – grows stronger the closer I get to the two. It intrigues me, but the instinct to protect my Alpha and sworn sister overrides any thoughts I may have.

"Caden, let go." I stop, my heart beat pausing for a split second with anxiety as I realize this voice is Amelia's. I can see the two wolves now through the branches and watch as she pulls at a hand, trying to free herself from the male's grasp.

"I will when we get to the cave." The male retorts with his deep voice, carrying a hint of exasperation as he pulls Amelia towards my direction. I suppress my growl, wanting to tear into this male for being so close to her and not releasing her like she demanded. Who does he think he is?

Amelia growls in response, and I catch the male wince before he quickly lets Amelia go. The scent of blood fills the air, and my anger grows fiercer at the thought of Amelia being injured. Without a second thought, I rush towards the male as he turns to reprimand Amelia, tackling him to the ground and placing my mouth around the back of his neck with my sharp teeth pressing against his fragile skin. One wrong move and I will end him.

He twitches, and I snarl, my one and only warning to the male that I will kill him if he tries anything. Amelia's scent fills my nose before the soft touch of her hand is felt running through my fur. I stop snarling, allowing a quick glance her way to see if I can spot any wounds. Thankfully, I don't see anything, not even a mark on her neck.

"Grace, he isn't going to hurt me." My friend states in a whisper, laying her head against my shoulder. I blink, releasing the male's neck from my hold, but keep a paw pressed to the small of his back. My ears twitch, letting Amelia know that I am listening to her while I keep an eye out for any strange movement the male might make.

"Grace, Caden has been helping me find you and keeping me safe from other wolves. You can trust him." She continues, her fingers still running through my fur. I eye the male suspiciously, removing my paw from his back before nodding to Amelia. I trust her judgement, and now that I am slightly calmer, I notice the wound on the male's wrist where the scent of blood from early pools. It seems my friend injured this male wolf in some way, and pride swells inside me.

"I don't think she trusts me yet." The male states quietly, looking over his shoulder at Amelia. My lips curl back in a warning snarl, and I remind the male that I am the one in control as I place my paw back onto the small of his back, allowing my claws to slightly poke him.

"She is just protecting me. We are sworn sisters, and to her, you are a male that might claim me." Amelia states, rubbing the top of my head. I nod, agreeing with her words, and the male lets out a sigh of defeat, turning his head to expose his neck to me in surrender. Shocked, I once again move my paw from his body as I allow Amelia to wrap her arms around my neck and hug me, placing her head on my shoulder.

[I trust him, Grace.] Amelia sends through our link; truth mixed with exhaustion laced in her words. I pause for a moment, debating on if I should move or not and allow the male to get up.

[Are you sure, Amelia? I don't want him harming either of us.] I ask, sighing slightly while nuzzling my friend gently.

[He won't hurt us. Trust me, Grace.] She answers reassuringly. I take a moment to let her words sink in before slowly backing away and sitting down just a foot away from the male. Taking a deep breath to calm my racing heart, the male's scent rushes into my body, and my tail wags slightly. I could get used to his scent of a fresh forest on a winter's day.

"I'm Caden-" I growl when this male interrupts my thoughts as he stands, his body moving towards mine. My growl stops him in his tracks, and he looks to Amelia for help, but the blonde just shrugs helplessly. The male, Caden, will have to earn my trust before I allow him near me, even if he smells delectable to me.

"I guess you are not in a trusting mood still, Lady Silver." He mumbles sheepishly, rubbing the back of his head. I huff, ignoring the fact that he has given me a nickname, and look at Amelia.

[Follow me, the cave we agreed to meet at is just ahead.] I link her before standing and turning back in the direction I came from. I take a few steps forward as Amelia lets out a chuckle, my ears twitching at her voice. I am so relieved to see her safe and sound, but more intrigued by why a male is traveling with her.

"She wants us to follow her to a cave." Amelia states to Caden with another chuckle. My ears twitch once more to the sound of the two wolves following behind me. They are quiet, their footsteps barely audible, and I smile. At least Caden has some common sense not to make noise when traveling, especially with daybreak being only minutes away.

[Tell him that I want to shift and put on clothes before he enters the cave.] I link Amelia again as we grow closer to the cave entrance. She relays my message the moment I duck under the ledge and pad inside, the cool stone making me think that it would be nice to sleep here in wolf form to stay warm, but I also need to talk to this male Caden.

I shift back into my skin form, taking a moment to stretch my sore body, then quickly dress. Once I am properly clothed, I lean against the stone wall behind me on the opposite side to the cave entrance and take a deep breath.

[You can come in now.] I link Amelia once I am mentally prepared to face Caden. Their steps echo into the cave soon afterwards, and I do my best to look calm and collected.

Amelia comes into view first, her small form bounding towards me where she promptly throws her arms around my neck and hugs me tight, my arms instinctively wrapping around the shorter she-wolf as my eyes soften.

"I am so glad I found you." She whimpers out. I can sense the fear in her words, and my heart cracks. We are sworn sisters, being the only child in our respective families. With cruel fathers, Amelia and I trained side by side, always protecting each other.

"I am glad you found me, too. Do you still have the token on?" I whisper out, taking in her scent.

"I do, but we haven't run into any Fae yet." Relieved by her words, I tell her to get some rest on the mattress in the cave. Her eyes have dark circles around them, and I can tell that the last few days, from being drugged and caged to having to walk through the forest, have been hard on her. She complies thankfully, walking over to the mattress and climbing onto it. It doesn't take long for Amelia to fall asleep, and I smile softly, relieved that I can interrogate this male without my friend interrupting us. I need to make sure this wolf is safe and has no other ulterior motives for helping Amelia.

Turning away from my sleeping friend, I look at the male who has been patiently waiting for Amelia and me to finish our reunion and nod. At least he is respectful.

"You said your name is Caden?" I ask, taking in his slightly disheveled appearance.

"Yes, Ma'am." He answers promptly. I sniff the air and notice he is speaking the truth. Good. I prefer talking to honest wolves.

"Who are you, Caden?" I demand, my sapphire eyes staring into his own as I allow the power in my blood to radiate off of me. I am weary of this unmated male, weary of how close he is to Amelia. I can see he is thinking over his words, probably in order not to anger me. At least this male is smart.

Chapter 16 Caden

―――

"Grace, he isn't going to hurt me." I hear Amelia say in a low whisper to Grace as she does her best to calm the angry she-wolf down. I keep as still as possible, not wanting to make any sudden movements that may end with sharp canines tearing my neck apart, and remind myself to stay as calm as I can with a large, deadly, and powerful she-wolf above me. I wince as she growls, her teeth grazing my skin uncomfortably, but she isn't going for the kill - yet.

Thankfully, it seems that Amelia is able to calm Grace slightly as the sharp teeth retreat from my neck and the powerful pressure of an Alpha wolf that has been radiating towards me pulls back, giving me space to breathe. Who knew that Grace could have so much power in her blood that it could cause even me to have a hard time breathing.

"Grace, Caden has been helping me find you and keeping me safe from other wolves. You can trust him." Amelia continues, putting a good word in for me. I thank the Goddess that I met Amelia first and have been keeping her safe for the last twenty-four hours. Without her, I don't think I would be left uninjured if I had met Grace alone.

I suppress the chuckle that wants to leave my lips when I think about how I met Amelia, the blonde tackling me to the ground and threatening me just like Grace is right now. I can see why these two are close, as they are similar in how they treat unknown males.

"I don't think she trusts me yet." I state quietly, looking over my shoulder at Amelia. Grace's lips curl back in a warning snarl and remind me that, in this moment, with her paw being placed back onto my back and the sharp claws poking into my skin, she is the one in control.

"She is just protecting me. We are sworn sisters, and to her, you are a male that might claim me." Amelia states, rubbing the top of Grace's head. Grace nods, agreeing with her friend's words, and I let out a sigh of defeat. If I want Grace to trust me, then I have to submit to her right now.

Turning my head to expose my neck, I surrender to Grace and hope that she sees that I am no threat to her. A few seconds later, I feel her move away from me and breathe a sigh of relief. Amelia and my actions must have shown her that I am no threat. I slowly move into a sitting position to spot Amelia throwing her arms around Grace, the small blonde nearly being buried by the long flowing silver fur. My breath catches in my throat as I stand, and I wonder how beautiful Grace must be in skin form as her sapphire eyes look at Amelia with love and relief.

"I'm Caden-" She growls again when I try to introduce myself, making me stop in my tracks from walking towards her. I have a feeling that until she gets to know me, her guard will be up, and I may end up like that male by the tree a few kilometers back from the way we came.

"I guess you are not in a trusting mood, still, Lady Silver." I mumble out sheepishly, looking away as I rub the back of my head. She really is a strong and powerful wolf, and I cannot wait to earn her trust and get to know her.

Grace closes her eyes for a moment before she abruptly stands and walks away. Amelia chuckles before turning to me with an apologetic smile, while I look at her with a questioning gaze. It seems these two have been linking the whole time, and all I can hope is that it was Amelia putting a good word in for me.

"She wants us to follow her to a cave." Amelia states with another chuckle. I nod, deciding that staying quiet right now is the right thing to do with Grace still untrusting of me and daylight being so close. We can't risk other wolves hearing us before we make it to safety. We keep to the shadows of the trees as the sky lightens with each minute that passes until the entrance of a cave appears. Grace pads in first, and I go to follow, but Amelia stops me.

"She wants to shift and change into clothes first." My friend states, giving me an apologetic smile.

"I guess she wants to interrogate me?" I ask quietly, deciding to take a step back and lean against a tree. Amelia sighs, neither denying my words nor confirming them. It seems even she knows her sworn sister wants to question my intentions, and I can't blame her. A lone male traveling with an unmated female is questionable in The Run, and most males would use this tactic to gain the trust of a she-wolf before claiming her just near the end of the event. I just hope I can prove that the only other motive I have is to take Grace on a few dates and get to know her outside of The Run.

"We can enter now." Amelia says quietly, breaking me from my thoughts. Amelia rushes in first, and I follow, emerging inside the cave just in time to see Amelia run towards Grace and into her arms. I watch the heart-warming scene of the two girls hugging one another, their eyes misty with unshed tears, and lean against the wall beside the entrance to give them their moment.

"I am so glad I found you." Amelia whimpers. I can sense the fear in her words from my spot and sigh inwardly. Amelia was so scared, and even though I helped her, I know I couldn't ease the fear the way her best friend could.

"I am glad you found me, too. Do you still have the token on?" Grace whispers back. Her voice is soft – almost musical – with a hint of love and affection. My heart skips a beat, not understanding how someone could have such a captivating voice that I could listen to all day and never get tired of hearing it. She has this magnetic pull, one that calls to me, and I realize in this moment how screwed I am if I can't control myself.

"I do, but we haven't run into any Fae yet," Amelia mumbles, taking me out of my thoughts. I wonder what they mean by token and why it would involve the Fae, but I decide it is another question for later as Grace tells Amelia to get some rest. Her care and love for the blonde she-wolf reminds me of how

I treat my little sister, and I smile. I hope Karina is safe and okay at the Lodge and that there haven't been too many wolves rescued from the forest and sent her way.

Grace watches Amelia until she is fast asleep, her warm gaze one I hope to gain in the future while I wait silently for her to interrogate me. Once Amelia is deep in her slumber, her gaze turns to me, and her soft smile turns into a hard, icy glare.

"You said your name is Caden?" She asks, her captivating voice holding a hint of distrust.

"Yes, Ma'am." I answer promptly, keeping my words respectful and only speaking the truth. This seems to please the she-wolf as her glare softens, and I hold in my sigh of relief. So far, so good.

"Who are you, Caden?" She demands the power in her blood radiating off of me. I think over my words, trying to decide how to speak the truth without sharing my identity. I don't want to deceive her, but I also don't want anyone to know who I truly am.

"Caden Wolfrain, from Wœlf Haven and future Alpha." I state honestly, running a hand through my hair. It is not a lie, as Wœlf Haven was my mother's pack, and I inherited it from her as she has no living relatives. Right now, the Beta is the acting Alpha, and as soon as I take my rightful place from my father, I plan to merge the two packs. Grace seems shocked by my answer as a look of recognition fills her eyes. There is another name I go by, one known to she-wolves in The Run.

"The Golden Boy, friend to she-wolves at The Run." She whispers, and I nod. At twenty-four, I have participated in The Run for six years, a total of twelve events as of today. After watching Felix claim Linda, I knew I could never do that and started helping she-wolves who did not want to be mated, sending them on the safest routes and showing them how to avoid the Fae, lust-filled males, and Ragers.

"Yes, that's me." I confirm, her gaze softening some more as she looks at me with a questioning gaze.

"Why are you here again? You haven't claimed a mate and always help she-wolves. Aren't you tired of coming to The Run?" She asks, and I sigh. I look away and smile as Amelia turns in her sleep while mumbling something. Grace sees my action and does the same, letting out a chuckle.

"I was forced to come to The Run by my father. If I don't take a mate the old-fashioned way, then I lose my title as heir..." I mumble out my words, slowly growing hard and trailing off as I think about my father and Felix. I hated them both. Hated their treatment of the she-wolves in the pack and how they both abused their mates. It's no wonder that my father loves Felix more than me.

"And if you don't, then someone else you hate takes it and possibly ruins your pack." She finishes, and I nod. It seems she is starting to trust me more and more with our short conversation.

"Who is he?" She asks as she walks over to my direction, where a bag sits. I didn't notice it before as she rummaged through it and motioned for me to sit as she brought out a container. I sit down, happy to let my legs relax after a long night of walking, and settle in as Grace takes a spot beside me, offering me the beef jerky and dried fruit she has taken out. I thank her, taking a bite of the jerky before answering.

"My cousin Felix. Vilest man you will ever meet. He raped his mate and beats her daily before heading into the cities to fuck unsuspecting humans or even just finding a few pack whores from the pack to play with. Linda doesn't deserve it." I sigh and take another angry bite of my jerky.

"He sounds like he needs to be stopped." Grace scoffs out, taking a bite of the dried fruit – apple, if I am not mistaken – and I nod in agreement.

"If he becomes Alpha, then my pack will die from his reign. But I plan to do something about this at the lodge. I can't let my father and Felix ruin our pack further." I state.

"Do you plan to challenge your father?" She questions, and I nod, my gaze filled with hatred as I look at the wall where Grace once leaned against moments earlier.

"I plan to kill him and maybe even Felix." Grace just nods at my words, her silence all that I need to know that she doesn't judge me for my plan. If anything, I think she respects me for it and for how I plan to put a stop to their terror.

"Amelia is in a similar situation. Her father is a complete ass, and if she doesn't step up as Alpha soon, the pack will fall." Grace states. I already know the situation, Amelia confiding in me that she hopes Grace wins the bet so that she can become Alpha and fix her pack. I know the she-wolf will become a great leader. I just hope that Amelia can forgive me if Grace and I end up together and I take the silver she-wolf away to be part of my own pack one day. That is, if I can ask the wolf beside me on a date and get to know her.

"I am Grace Harvest, by the way." Grace says, her words now warm and accepting of me.

"Amelia already told me all about you, Grace, and about your bet with her Father. If you don't mind, I would like to help you win it for both yours and Amelia's sakes." She smiles at my words before looking away with a blush and leaning her head on my shoulder. I am shocked by how fast I have earned her trust, but thank the Goddess nonetheless as I allow her to lean against me.

"I'd like that, Caden." I smile out as she lets out a yawn.

"And thank you for keeping Amelia safe." She mumbles quietly as she drifts off to sleep on my shoulder.

Chapter 17 Grace

———

*T*he soft breeze rolls past me, ruffling the heavy gown that is draped on my small frame as I stare out into the field of moon flowers. The Blue forest is our safe haven from them, from the wolves that want us dead. I sigh, looking towards the man I am in love with, his gold hair now cut short just like my silver hair. Easier to hide away behind trees without our long hair blowing in the wind and giving us away to our pursuers. I wonder if we will ever be left alone to fulfill our destiny as I watch my mate skin our kill, the hide to be made into a blanket for the winter...

My eyes open slowly as the dream fades away. It is the same woman and man from before, and I wonder who it is that has been sending them to me. Before, they were worried about The Run; now it seems these two wolves were on the run. Someone wanted them dead, but who?

I let out a sigh and decide to try and rest a little longer, letting my eyes fall shut once more. With Caden and Amelia here, it should be safe to sleep. I didn't expect the mattress to be this comfortable, but then, as I am about to let sleep take me once more, I notice that I am lying comfortably against something firmer than the mattress that Amelia had fallen asleep on last night. A strong yet gentle arm is wrapped around me, and the warmth from the body against mine calms me. I smile, thinking that I could get used to the scent of the forest in winter mingling with my mint and lavender.

"Okay, you cuddle bugs, the sun is setting, and it's time to move!" Amelia calls out, making me open my eyes to glare at her. The arm around me tightens, and a face is buried into my hair. In this moment, I become fully awake as I realize that I am in the arms of a male.

"I don't want to go to school, Mom." A deep voice mumbles out, his chest rumbling underneath me. My eyes widen as I realize I am lying on Caden, my silver hair sprawled out along his chest, and a blush creeps along my face. I have never been this close to a male before, not even when on my missions.

Taking a deep breath, I calm my beating heart and turn my head just enough to catch sight of his sleeping face and notice the stubble growing along his chin. I cannot deny how handsome Caden is and ignore the fluttering in my stomach.

"It's a good thing that school gets put on hold during the week of The Run." I state, chuckling and watching as his eyes - emerald green like the forest in summer - look into my sapphire ones in confusion before they widen as he notices our position.

"Hi." He whispers sheepishly, a blush forming on his cheeks. Letting out a giggle, I watch his blush deepen as he sends me a shy smile, something I did not expect coming from the Golden Boy.

"Hi." I reply back, getting off of him slowly so as not to put all my weight onto one spot and hurt Caden, then standing to my feet. I stretch, my sore muscles feeling refreshed after the much-needed sleep. Maybe having Caden with Amelia and me is a great thing; I can sleep knowing a male's scent is protecting us from others.

"How far do you reckon we have to travel in the forest?" Amelia asks as I scurry over to my bag to take out some food. Taking a bite of the jerky, I think for a moment and try to visualize the map we were forced to study as pups.

"I would say we should reach the lodge in another two days, three if we run into more fledglings and other wolves." I answer as soon as I realize that this cave is closest to the halfway point.

"That's not bad. I am guessing we are avoiding the middle?" Caden asks as he sits up, his voice gruff with sleep as he rubs his eyes.

"Yes. Most of the traps are in the middle, with some being deadly. There are also the Fae to consider and the lake." Amelia answers this time, and I nod, watching as my friend takes out her own food. We both have decided long ago we would take the longer path around the edges of the forest after coming to the river. Whether that means we meet with each other or not, the edge of the Goddess's forest is the best path for those not wanting to be claimed, while also making it to the lodge a minimum of six days.

Since tonight is the third night of The Run, we still have four more nights of the moon being blue. Meaning I have four more nights to make it to the lodge unmated to win the bet. If I am not there before the sun rises, then Amelia's father will win, and all wolves in Silver Birch will be forced to go to The Run in the future.

The three of us slink out of the cave unnoticed after taking time to eat our meager meal of jerky and dried fruit that I shared with the two, Amelia and I deciding to be on either side of Caden with him between us after we refill our canteens from the river. We are lucky that most wolves have gone through the middle, giving Caden and me time to get to know one another.

"So you have a half sister?" I ask, stepping onto a fallen log that lies across a narrow part of the river. Two hours have passed since we left the cave, and other than for a few she-wolves that are traveling at night as well, we haven't come across anyone else.

"Yeah. She was born a few years before my mom passed away to one of the pack whores. My father was pissed that the she-wolf gave birth to my sister instead of getting an abortion and killed the she-wolf in anger." Caden confesses. I frown, thinking about how unfair it is to be a she-wolf. Our lives are held at the mercy of a male, and at any moment, we may lose them if we anger any males.

"My mother helped protect my sister, and luckily, we were raised together." He continues with a small smile, his eyes brightening as he talks about his sister, who I now want to meet.

"What happened to your mother, if you don't mind me asking." I whisper quietly, seeing the sadness replace the brightness in his emerald green eyes.

"He beat her to death as well. I was fifteen at the time, and she was tired of the abuse. I guess walking into their room after negotiating a treaty to find him buried deep in one of her so-called friends was the straw that broke her." The sadness in his eyes turns to anger, and I watch as his fists clench. I think back to my own mother and what the ladies of the pack told me about her. She died giving birth to me, her body weak from the beatings received from my father. How she had spent a short four years of misery with my father before birthing me took her life.

"I am sorry." That's all I manage to squeak out after awkward silence settles between us, far longer than needed.

"You remind me of her." He chuckles out, his green eyes looking into my sapphire ones. My mouth opens to say something, but the sound of a long, slow howl causes a shiver to run down my spine. Our foot steps pause, and Amelia moves closer to me, our eyes meeting for a brief moment. Taking a deep breath, I open my senses, feeling Caden shift closer to the two of us as I try to locate the source of the howl. When I do, I instantly realize how fucked we are.

"We need to move, now!" I state with urgency, taking Amelia's hand and veering to the right.

"What did you find?" Caden asks, his eyes scanning the trees as we rush forward. Our initial idea of traveling on the edge of the forest is gone; the wolves I scented made sure of that. They were spread out an equal distance, slowly moving towards the centre of the forest, and in our direct path. If we do not find a place to hide soon, Amelia and I will be in trouble.

"Three wolves heading towards us. All are male and from their similar scents I would say rogue from the same band." I answer quietly. I think about where we can hide and how to mask out scents.

"How far away?" Amelia inquires, her eyes also scanning the trees while her hand tightens its grasp in mine.

"Twenty minutes out, but I believe they are in their fur forms." I reply, trying to frantically search my memories of The Run for a hiding spot that will protect us. Amelia takes the lead as she tells me to heighten my senses and see if I can find their intent. Caden looks at us in confusion, but I ignore his gaze and close my eyes. I trust Amelia to guide me safely while I allow my senses to expand, and I search for the three wolves.

I see them in my mind, their forms a blur, but their intent is clear. These wolves radiate pure hunt and lust. I shiver, my steps faltering, and I feel strong arms keeping me from tripping while I continue to assess the males tracking us. One howls, forcing me to open my eyes as I look to my companions.

"We need to shift." I state, dropping my bag from my shoulders and stripping, not caring if Caden can see my naked body. Amelia follows my lead, with Caden pausing before removing his clothes as well.

"What did you see?" Amelia asks.

"Ragers, and they are tracking us, Amelia." She gasps, quickly stuffing her clothing into her pack while I do the same for mine. I know we will be unable to communicate with Caden in our fur form, but our survival depends on us shifting.

"There should be a small creek that leads to a lake. It's closer to the middle of the forest, but there is a cave behind a waterfall that not many know about." Caden says. I am shocked at this knowledge, knowing about the waterfall but not that there is a cave behind it. If we are lucky, the Ragers may not know about this.

"You lead the way then. Amelia, I want you to stay close to Caden." I order, cutting off any of her protests when I zip my bag shut and shift. Amelia sighs before accepting my order, and soon her blonde wolf stands before me. A golden wolf nudges my shoulder, and I turn to see the familiar emerald green eyes of Caden staring at me. I walk towards him, pushing my snout into his flank to memorize his scent in case we are separated, then motion for the male to take the lead.

He surprised me by burying his face into the crook of my neck, his breath brushing against my fur before backing away and yipping. Picking up his pack in his teeth, he trots away into the trees, and Amelia follows with her pack in her grasp. I falter for a moment; my heart fluttering, and I realize I just may lose the bet if I allow this golden-haired wolf to get closer to me. Shaking my fur, I pick up my pack and catch up to the two wolves.

True to Caden's words, he leads us to a creek just a ten-minute run to the east from the center of the forest. Thankful for the water flowing downstream, and we all pad into the cool stream and continue trotting away from our pursuers.

I pray to the Goddess that we make it to safety before the Ragers can catch up to us.

Chapter 18 Caden

———

I keep my eyes trained on the forest around us while also keeping Grace and Amelia within my sight. Ragers are bad news. No one knows how their Rogue community started, but every pup in an established pack is warned about Ragers and their goals. Ragers are Rogues, either born to the community or banished from a pack for a variety of reasons – the main reason usually being treason to their Alpha. Once a Rogue becomes a Rager, they spend their days building their Rogue pack through rape and pillaging.

Usually, in The Run, they are hunting down she-wolves, bringing them to their community, and using the poor she-wolf as a breeding tool. She may bear the mark of one of the wolves, but the community will each take a turn with her. A male will wait for the captured she-wolf to bear a pup and her body just healed enough before he takes his turn raping her, breeding her until she is pregnant once more. A she-wolf in a Rager community is nothing but a pup making factory until her body is spent, and death is the final outcome.

If the three pursuing us are to catch up, their target will first be me, as they will want to eliminate any male guarding a she-wolf, whether that she-wolf is mated or not. Then they will capture Amelia and Grace and take them to where their fellow wolves hide. If this happens, then any hope of seeing Grace or Amelia again will be gone.

The sound of falling water is soon heard and just in time as Grace, Amelia, and I take a leap of fate and jump straight into the lake I am leading them to. Grace is fast, her silver fur looking like a fish as she swims past me and towards the waterfall. I slow and allow Amelia to follow her friend before I, too, swim around the falling water and climb onto the small ledge just behind the curtain of safety the waterfall provides. Amelia and Grace are waiting for me at the cave entrance with their bags still hanging from their mouths, and I motion for the two of them to go further in, which they thankfully do.

We walk quietly deeper into the cave, making sure not to make too much noise in case the rushing water does not drown out any sound we make until the sounds of the water fade and nothing but silence remains. We need to shift soon to be able to communicate, but we have yet to make it to the small cavern that I usually use as my base during The Run.

Grace slows her pace, allowing Amelia to take the lead as she comes to walk beside me, her damp fur brushing against mine. Our eyes meet, and she nudges my shoulder gently. I get the feeling she is saying thank you.

Without thinking, I nuzzle her cheek, careful not to hit my bag against her, happy that she is trusting me in such a short time. Her steps falter, and I inwardly chuckle. It seems I affect this feisty she-wolf.

Our walk comes to an end when the tunnel we have been walking in opens to the small cavern. It seems no one else has been here, as the slight dust causes the three of us to sneeze, and I instantly regret not telling a trusted wolf to come in and keep the cavern clean. Amelia is the first to set her pack down and shift while Grace pads around the cave, her sapphire eyes taking in the two mattresses, the small love seat, and the chest. Hopefully, no creatures have gotten in and ruined the blankets I keep in there.

Setting my bag down, I shift and rummage through the chest, happy to see the four blankets still intact. I take three out, draping one over my shoulder before handing one to Amelia, careful to avoid looking at her body. Grace pads over, my hands itching to run through her damp fur, and I drape a blanket over her body. I watch as the blanket moves, the sounds of bones shifting coming from underneath until her head emerges.

"This cave has your scent all over it." She states quietly, standing from the floor and tightening the blanket around her.

"Yeah, it's my base here when I help she-wolves." I answer, shrugging. Rummaging through the chest once again, I grin when I find what I am looking for, taking out three cans of beef ravioli, three spoons, and a can opener. I check the dates, happy to know that the food has yet to expire, and give myself an imaginary pat on the back for remembering to place food in here six months ago.

"Anyone up for something other than jerky and dried fruit?" I ask with a smile, showing the cans to the girls. Amelia is the first to cheer, her little body rushing to my side and claiming a can that she promptly opens before returning with her prize to the mattress she had claimed. Grace chuckles, watching the blonde with amusement before turning to me.

"Thank you for sharing your cave with us, Caden." Her voice is soft, and so is her gaze as she takes the offered can of ravioli that I had just finished opening.

"You're welcome, Lady Silver." I whisper back, smiling when her fingers graze against mine. She takes her can of food and a spoon to the love seat, climbing onto the soft cushions and digging into her meal as soon as she is comfortable. Taking my own can, I join Grace on the love seat, and the three of us enjoy our meal in silence.

"What do we do now?" Amelia asks, the first to finish her ravioli.

"I say wait it out in Caden's cave for an hour, then take a chance through the middle of the forest." Grace chimes in before I can say anything. I nod, taking a bite of my food as I think of a plan.

"There are Fae in the middle and the large lake that no one knows much about." I add, setting my half-empty can on the arm of the love seat and walking to the chest once more. I open the hidden compartment on the side, Grace and Amelia watching my movement with curiosity as I bring out a folded sheet of paper and place it between all of us on the floor. Opening the paper, I reveal the map of the forest, which is outdated by about one and a half years, but it is better than nothing.

"As far as I am aware, new traps have been added here, here, and here." I sigh, pointing at three areas close to the center of the map where the lake is.

"What about the middle of the lake?" Amelia asks, pointing to the small island.

"As far as we are aware, nothing is inside the island. It's just a dead-end cave. Besides, the only way to get into it is either by swimming or using a boat." Amelia nods, accepting my answer, while Grace climbs off the love seat to kneel beside me and the map. She points at the red X on the map, her right brow raised in a silent question.

"Where we are now." I answer.

"Should we worry about how you got this map?" She asks, and I shrug.

"Took it off of a Rager a few years ago and just added to it over the years." I say, turning to look at the paper as I do my best to lie. I don't want her to know the truth of how I have this map; it might change her perspective of me if she were to learn the truth.

"Doesn't surprise me. Those wolves have some form of connection when it comes to illegal items." Grace sighs, crossing her legs as she sits comfortably on the ground.

"In about an hour, we should run in this part of the forest. Of course, we will be near the Fae, so stealth is required –"

"Just stick with Grace and me. Fae won't bother you." Amelia cuts me off with a smirk, pulling her hair back and revealing the gold earring on her ear. Grace chuckles and copies her movement, revealing the matching earring as the two she-wolves look at each other with a hint of mischief.

"Are those -"

"Tokens, yes. I received one for Amelia and me from the Faerie princess years ago." Grace confirms, a smile on her face.

"If I am not mistaken, she should be here now, so if we run into her, we will be fine." She adds as an afterthought. I finally understand what the earrings were for and why they mentioned the Fae last night. It seems that just as I get to know these two, they find a way to surprise me.

"Then I guess as long as we avoid the Ragers and make it near the Fae, the middle of the forest will be easy for us."

Chapter 19 Grace

———

I sit at the entrance of the cave, the sound of rushing water drowning out anything the quiet night may hide. My eyes are closed, and as I take a deep breath, I open my senses to the surroundings and search for any wolves near us. Nothing appears out of the ordinary, and no wolves are near us, meaning now is as good a chance as any for our group to advance further into the forest.

"We should be good to run soon." I state, opening my eyes and turning back to look at Caden in his golden wolf form and Amelia with her blonde fur slightly damp from the mist of the waterfall. His green eyes meet mine, and I quickly turn away, hoping that I am not blushing as I stand and drop the blanket that is covering me. I shift quickly, my bones realigning themselves until I stand in my fur form. Two hours have passed since we came to hide in Caden's den, meaning we lost time waiting out the Ragers, and now we need to gain it back by executing our plans.

Picking up my bag in my mouth, I nod to my companions before jumping into the water and padding towards the shore with the sounds of Caden and Amelia following me as they both splash into the water. I roll my eyes, thinking that Amelia will need more training later when it comes to swimming in wolf form once we return home, and I refocus on swimming to the other side. I glide under the water, careful to keep my movement smooth and create as little noise as possible. As soon as I find myself on land, I shake the water from my fur while I wait for the other two to join me. My senses are alert to every movement while I look around for any potential threat, knowing we are vulnerable right now.

Caden is the first to reach the shore, his emerald eyes staring into mine before the splashing of Amelia joining us pulls his attention away. She too shakes the water from her fur before she pads to my side, nudging her head affectionately against my shoulder.

With the three of us now on solid land, we take off into the forest with Caden in the lead and Amelia and me flanking his sides. We will need to make it close to the Fae before morning to find a place to rest. If I am not mistaken, there will be more caves and tree houses for us to sleep in, but this also means there will be more wolves to contend with.

Caden skillfully leads us through the forest, and once again, I am thankful that this wolf has been to The Run multiple times. His knowledge of the land is a blessing to Amelia and me, and hopefully, we will reach the lodge without any more problems because of Caden and his help. Caden slows his run, his hackle raised as he stares to the left. I shudder, closing my eyes and taking a deep breath.

[Grace, what's wrong?] Amelia asks through our link. I ignore her question for the time being as Caden looks back at me. I can see the worry and fear in his eyes and know instantly that we underestimated the Ragers. He nods, as if sensing my own fear and drops his bag to shift.

"We are too far from the waterfall, but there is a cave just a few meters away. If we can make it there, Amelia and you will be safe." He states as soon as he is back to his skin side. I nod, understanding his meaning and wait for Caden to shift back to his wolf form and lead the way once more. He takes us slightly to the right, always checking back to see if Amelia and I are following, while howls of wolves on a hunt sound around us. The Ragers have scented us, but there is a chance we can find safety soon.

The trees around us grow denser, making it impossible for Amelia and me to run on either side of Caden. Instead, we are left to continue our escape in a single line with Caden in the lead, Amelia behind him, and me taking the rear. I can hear the Ragers, but the forest is too dense for them to get to us, and I smile. Once again, we escaped from their pursuit.

Time passes with the three of us slowly trotting in a single file line until the trees begin to clear up, and soon we find ourselves in a meadow of moon flowers hidden in the forest by a dense wall of trees. Caden drops his bag, padding into the meadow and dropping onto his stomach, where he promptly rolls around the flowers like a little pup before abruptly stopping and shifting to his skin form.

"Roll in the flowers to hide your scent. It's going to be morning soon, so we should get some rest." Caden calls out before lying back on the soft meadow. I drop my bag on the ground beside his before finding a spot to roll around in. The soft, fragrant scent of the moon flowers fills my senses, calming me. Something about this field seems familiar, as if I have been here before. With a soft smile and now fully covered in the moon flower's scent, I decide to rest where I am and stretch out on the ground, my tail wagging gently.

"Comfy?" Amelia asks, laughing. In her hand is my pack, and she smiles when placing it in front of me.

[Is it that obvious?] I ask, resting my head on my paws while Amelia takes a seat beside me, running her fingers through my fur.

"Yes. But you and I both know we need to talk about how we are going to get passed the Ragers." Closing my eyes, I take in her words and know Amelia is right, but I don't want Amelia to be in danger. She has Bryden waiting for her safe return, while I have no one but Amelia. I cannot allow her to be claimed or captured by anyone, especially Ragers, when she has someone to return to. Shifting to my skin, I stretch my limbs and dress quickly. I know what needs to be done to protect Amelia, and that means I need to wait for her to be asleep before I can speak to Caden.

"Let's rest like Caden suggested, then we can come up with a plan when we wake up."

Chapter 20 Caden

———

A soft smile graces my lips as I watch Amelia and Grace, the blonde girl and silver wolf, making a great sight. I understand why Amelia wanted to find Grace when we first met - the two make a great team and always seem to be on the same wavelength. I want to tell them that we are closer to the halfway point than they think, that if we were to walk behind this cave to the other side of the meadow, we would be in Fae territory. But the chances of the Fae keeping my secret from the girls are slim to none.

"Penny for your thoughts?" I look up to see Grace looking at me with a smile, her sapphire eyes warm and bright. She must have shifted when I was lost in thought, her arm looped through Amelia's, but I can see she has something to say.

"Thanks, but I think we should keep that lucky penny tucked away until we can figure out a way out of this mess." I stammer out, Amelia giving me a sly look before turning to Grace.

"I am going to get some sleep. We've been running from Ragers for hours, and I am exhausted." She states, taking Grace's bag from her. Before she enters the cave, Amelia gives me a wink, and I have the sinking feeling that she is trying to set me up with her best friend.

"Do you also want to sleep?" I ask Grace, her sapphire eyes watching her friend disappear safely inside before turning to look at me with a sigh.

"No. We need to talk." She answers, taking my hand. I feel like my stomach is turning with thousands of butterflies as she leads me away from the cave. We walk in silence, Grace turning to look back at the cave every so often until we are on the far end of the meadow.

"She shouldn't be able to hear me – us – from here." I try my best to hide my frown when she releases my hand to run her fingers through her hair while pacing in front of me.

"What's wrong, Grace?" I ask, torn between wanting to pull her into my arms and letting her pace away the agitation I feel radiating off of her.

"The Ragers." She growls out, stopping in front of me once again. Her sapphire eyes stare into mine, and the anger and fear hidden inside those orbs have me pulling her into my arms and wanting nothing more than to take those fears away.

"You and I know that once they find a female, they will hunt her till the end of The Run until they can claim them. If we cannot stop them, they will take Amelia." Her voice starts quivering and he body shakes against mine. The worry and fear for her best friend are clear in her voice, and I hold her closer.

"She is my only family. She has Bryden. I-" Her voice cracks, and so does my heart as I instinctively run my fingers through her messy hair. The silver locks are tangled and dirty from the last few days spent in the forest.

"We won't let anyone hurt Amelia." I reassure her, pulling back far enough away to look into her tear-filled eyes. I hate to admit it, but even with tears on her face and watery, wide eyes, she looks beautiful.

"There is only one thing I can think of doing Caden." She whispers as I wipe the stray tears away from her face.

"And what's that, Grace?" I ask, my voice also a whisper.

"We need to take care of them before it's too late." She says, her voice leaving no room for any arguments.

Chapter 21 Grace

W atching Amelia sleep comfortably on the mattress, I let out a sad sigh. After my breakdown earlier while held in Caden's arms, I realized just how serious the situation we are in has become. I can not allow anyone to hurt her, to claim Amelia. I may have made a bet with her father, but Amelia is my chosen Alpha. The need to protect her over winning a bet is the most important thing to me right now.

"She'll be safe here, right?" I ask Caden, my eyes never leaving the girl I call my sister. She has Bryden waiting for her, while I only have her. If me being hurt means she can go home to him is what I must do, then I must do it.

"Yes. There is only one way in and one way out." Caden answers, easing my anxiety slightly.

"Besides, the moon flowers mask our scent, so no one will be able to locate us here." He continues quietly. His words are reassuring, and I place the note I had written explaining to Amelia the plan and that in the event I do not return, to go searching for the Fae. The Fae will help her cross the forest safely with the token on her, indicating she is an ally.

Standing, I turn to Caden with pleading eyes, hoping that if anything happens to me, he will protect my best friend. I remember the first time I learned about Ragers, being stuck in the Alpha's study with Amelia to learn about the dangers of The Run. We were twelve at the time, only six years away from being able to participate in the event, when I stumbled across them in a book. It was then that the two of us learned that Ragers are rogues that left their pack for a variety of reasons. Some are because they do not conform to pack life, some due to the death of a loved one. But the main reason is their betrayal of their pack and Alpha. They all share a similar belief, with one being taking as many she-wolves as they can to strengthen and grow their nomadic packs until they can legally claim land. There is nothing that a Rager wants more than power and to be stronger. The one page that stood out after reading about Ragers is the warning listed at the end.

If you see any Ragers, run.

If they find you, fight.

If you are claimed, find a way to end your life before you are used till your death.

I sigh, wondering if I will have to take my own life if the plan fails.

When making our plan, Caden informed me we are closer to the middle, where the majority of the traps are built in the forest, even drawing a rough map of the area where the closest traps are to us and what we can use to trap and injure the Ragers without having to fight them. I would lead the chase, making sure the Ragers follow me, and Caden will trail behind, knocking the ones at the back into the traps one by one until none are left standing. Once all the Ragers are dealt with, we circle back to grab Amelia and our stuff and rush towards the Fae for safety and a much-needed rest before making a beeline to the lodge.

"We need to leave now if we want to be back before Amelia wakes." Caden urges me, nodding his head towards the cave exit. He is right. With night time waning and dawn approaching faster than ever, we need to leave the safety this meadow brings to take down the Ragers. Weakening them will be a win for the werewolf community.

We quietly leave the cave, deciding that shifting at the exit to the meadow before we go through the tunnel of trees is the safest way not to wake Amelia. I know if she were to find me missing, she would hunt me down once more, and I can't allow that.

"Trust in me, Grace, I will protect you." Caden's soft words break through the silence of the early dawn. My steps falter, and I turn my head slightly to my right to see him staring down at me, a soft smile on his face. My heart flutters and for a moment – just a brief moment – and I believe he will do everything he can to protect me.

Reaching the edge of the meadow where hours ago we emerged, Caden and I quickly remove our clothes and shift, with him taking the lead as once again we run through the tunnel of trees. I can hear them the farther we run – hear the Ragers howling in the early morning as they catch my scent.

They are ready to hunt, and their prey is me.

The tunnel comes to an end faster than I remember, and just as planned, Caden and I break off from each other. I head in the direction of the center of the forest, where the traps we will use to our advantage await. I can hear them behind me, their undeniable scent of mud and grass the marking of a Rager. They are drawing close, planning how to capture me and in this moment, I realize just how many Ragers there are hunting me. I can feel my heart pounding as six distinctive howls sound and an emotion I have not felt in a long time settles into the pit of my stomach.

I am scared.

Chapter 22 Caden

'*F*uck, *there are a lot more than the two from before.*' I think to myself, pissed off for not using the power in my blood and forcing a link between Grace and me.

I should have insisted on one to make it easier to communicate, but that would mean revealing my true self to her – something I am not yet ready to do. I fear that if she were to find out who I truly am, she would hate me and never give me the time of day again.

I keep a steady pace behind the six Ragers pursuing Grace, making sure to stay just far enough away that I go undetected. Even so, it seems that the Ragers only have their mind set on Grace. This is good. Even if I can scent her fear, with the Ragers clueless to me following behind, we can take care of them with ease. Thankfully, even with her fear, Grace is sticking to the plan. She is racing through the trees like a flash of silver light and always staying far from the Ragers' grasp. I wait patiently for her to bring them closer to the traps, any would be fine, but I prefer one that could kill these horrid wolves.

My eyes stay trained on the silver wolf and watch as she makes a sharp turn to the left, her indication that a trap is directly behind her. My paws instinctively push forward as I gain speed and wait for the perfect opportunity to perform my part of the plan. I watch the wolves scramble to turn and chase after Grace, giving me time to catch up to the ones ahead and slam my body into a scrawny black wolf. He yelps, his body flying into the ruddy brown wolf beside him and the two land on a seemingly simple patch of dirt. A crack sounds as the ruddy brown stands, and in an instant, the ground gives way. The two wolves vanish into a twelve-foot-deep pit, and I look over to see them lying on the cold ground, bloodied and battered. Two down, four to go.

Grace makes a long turn to the right, jumping over a fallen log with ease. I stare in awe at her beauty and – ironically – grace. She leads the Ragers in a cat and mouse chase, the four wolves behind her panting like mutts in heat. They can taste her fear in the air, but also the power in her blood, power that has left me in awe since meeting her. One day, she will make a powerful she-wolf, and I have a feeling that a Beta role is just too small for her.

Shaking my head and returning my focus to the task at hand, I watch just in time as Grace is able to make a veer to the right and smirk as one of the wolves is unable to keep up with her sharp turns and falls into another trap. The scent of blood floats from the pit this wolf fell into, and after a quick glance, I wince in empathy. Unfortunately for this wolf, tree roots have grown into the pit, and he has the shitty luck of being stabbed right through the leg with one. He will be out of commission for a while with the damage caused to his hind leg, and shifting to human form is out of the question for him.

Two of the three remaining Ragers split off from the group, their bodies disappearing into the dense forest surrounding us. Panic settles in, and I wonder if they are running to gather more support. Grace and I need to finish this lone wolf off now and rush back to Amelia and make our way to safety fast before the other two can bring more Ragers.

Grace continues to run, weaving through the trees, bushes and rocks without missing a step, her eyes searching the forest as I try to keep up with her and the lone Rager. Suddenly, the two wolves that had separated from the pursuit appear like ghosts in front of Grace, forcing her to skid to a stop and dodge their attack. The three wolves slowly take turns attacking her, forcing Grace to back into what I can only describe as a wall of stone. She growls, her fur standing on edge as the wolf in the middle, one I have concluded to be the leader of this small group, shifts to human. He is tall, at least five feet eleven inches, but his body is built of muscle.

"Now, now, beautiful." He coos, smiling at Grace, who eyes him with hatred.

"I think it's time you stop running and come with us willingly." The man chuckles out, his red hair blowing in the breeze. Grace snarls at him, baring her teeth, and I can tell she is ready to fight. I need to reach her fast if she is to be safe.

"You have spunk, silver wolf. Our Alpha will love you." The man states with a smirk as he reaches his hand out to touch her fur, only to snatch it back quickly when Grace lunges to attack. He curses, the scent of blood filling the air, and I chuckle. My Grace is a fighter, and this wolf just learned that the hard way.

The two wolves standing on either side of the man snarl back at Grace, not happy that their leader was injured, but the man holds his hand out to stop them. It seems they want Grace uninjured. The only reason that I can think of is that she will be left for their Alpha.

Threatened at the thought of Grace being saved to be claimed by a wolf before I can get to know her, I channel the power within my blood and surge forward. My first target is the brown wolf closest to me, his scrawny frame being an easy target. Without thinking, I am out of the safety of the trees and tackling the brown wolf. My jaw clenches around the scruff of his neck, and as if throwing a sack of grain, I toss this wolf into the nearest tree. Bones crack, and the wolf lies motionless at the base of the tree, thankfully still breathing.

A snarl has me turning around to see the black wolf lunging at me, his teeth sinking into the flesh of my shoulder. A whelp of pain escapes my throat, and I whirl around, using the same tree that I harmed his friend with to knock this black wolf off of me. A soft thud is heard, and the wolf thankfully lets go, leaving my shoulder bloodied and bruised.

"It seems we have a wolf trying to be a hero." The leader states with a chuckle, returning my attention to him. It seems that within the few moments I have been preoccupied with his two lackeys, another wolf had snuck up on us and now has an unconscious Grace on his shoulders. My lips furl back in a snarl while I draw closer. How did these wolves get their hands on her?

"Ah, ah, ah, Goldilocks. One more step, and I will have my friend here kill her." The leader chuckles as his friend holds a gun to Grace's head, reminding me that her life is now in their hands. What bothers me the most is that she is still in her wolf form. Any drug by now would have forced her to change into her human form, so what is stopping her?

"Curious about your friend here?" The leader asks, his grin growing. I growl, trying to figure out how I can get her away from these wolves.

"It's simple, a knock-out drug mixed with a bit of wolfsbane." Without warning, the gun is turned to me, and before I can dodge, I feel something embedding itself into my injured shoulder. I snarl, turning my head just far enough to see a dart sticking from my shoulder. The world begins to grow blurry, my limbs feeling weak and heavy.

"Now, I think we have been here long enough. Everyone is probably wondering when I will be back with our prizes." The man chuckles as more wolves emerge from the trees, some carrying an unconscious she-wolf in their arms. I lunge forward, not wanting to give up fighting, but my legs give out. The leader chuckles at my futile attempts, his beady eyes looking into mine as he runs his hands through Grace's fur.

"Don't worry, Goldilocks, we will take special care of this one. She will be the perfect Luna to our Alpha and the perfect breeder for our pack." With his taunting words, my eyes grow heavy, and as they close, I watch the wolves disappear.

I have failed to protect Grace.

Chapter 23 Grace

———

Darkness.

All that surrounds my heavy body is darkness, and I welcome it like a good friend. My mind is hazy, like a film thrown over my head, and I wonder if anyone will notice if I slip back into the dead sleep I was unwillingly waking up from. Sleep is something I haven't had enough of in the last few days, and right now I just wanted to escape into its blissful embrace.

"Shut your mouth, you little bitch!" A voice shouts, cutting through the darkness. I groan, frustrated by the person interrupting my sleep. Don't they know you should be quiet when someone in the room is asleep?

"I've claimed you, so take it like the whore you'll be." The voice continues, causing a rumble of a growl to vibrate from my chest. I open my eyes to find the source of the voice, spying various she-wolves chained to the wall behind them, some naked and some clothed only in a shirt and panties. My hazy mind takes a moment to realize what is happening until the events from earlier float through my mind.

I had been captured by the Ragers, and some time must have passed since then. Did Amelia wake up and find my note? Did she run to the Fae?

"I said shut up!" A loud slap cuts through my racing thoughts, and my eyes search for the source once more. Finally, I find the culprit of the yelling - a male pinning a small blonde she-wolf down on the ground, her hands tied to a pole in front of her as her naked body is bent uncomfortably forward. I watch as the male takes her from behind, his naked body covering her's as he grunts, thrusting himself inside her with pleasure contorting his face.

"Please, let me go!" The she-wolf begs, with a tear-stained face, only to scream as the male grabs a fistful of her hair and pulls her closer to him.

"You're mine, slut. As such, I will fuck you until you are pregnant." He growls, pushing her head onto the ground. A dull thud is heard from her head hitting the cold stone floor of the room – no, not a room but a cave. The she-wolf sobs quietly, her fate sealed as the man continues to fuck her heedlessly like an animal. The only sound in the cave is the male raping the poor wolf, the other she-wolves looking away in fear and staying silent in hopes of not being his next victim.

A growl rises in my throat, anger filling me at how barbaric these women are being treated. The man stops as I glare at him, letting the low, threatening growl escape past my lips as I carefully stand. It is now that I realize I am still in wolf form. The male chuckles, giving a final thrust into the girl with satisfaction, most likely finishing inside her, before pushing her away from him and leaving her battered and used body to heal from his assault.

"Hello, girly." He sneers, getting to his feet and slowly walking towards me. I growl out a warning, knowing that this man can be taken down in an instant as soon as he is in my reach. He chuckles, looking down at me as if I were a child. His cock is erect once more, and lust fills his eyes.

"I haven't had a she-wolf in wolf form yet. Care to be the first?" He asks, as he continues to move closer to me, his hand moving to stroke his cock, most likely thinking he will soon be penetrating me without problems. Furious, I lunge at the man, wanting to end his pathetic life, only to be yanked back and land on the ground hard. With the wind now knocked out of me, it dawns on me that I, too, am chained to the wall with a collar around my neck. I blame the drugs slowly weaning from my body for not noticing this detail sooner.

"What's all the commotion?" A man growls out as he walks into the room. Three others follow behind him. The man in front of me smiles, his hand moving faster as he rubs up and down his cock and nods in my direction.

"Little Silver here woke up and decided to growl at me." He answers with a chuckle as the others roll their eyes. I growl, standing to my feet and stepping closer to the wolf, wanting nothing more than to tear him limb from limb after he raped that poor girl. I strain against the chain securing me to my spot, trying my best to find a way to injure him. And then I see it.

"Remember, the boss wants her for himself." One of his companions sighs out with a chuckle, moving towards a dark skinned she-wolf with a dirty afro.

"But that doesn't mean you can't play with her." Someone else says as he chuckles.

"I know, maybe after he claims her I can -" His words are cut off by the blood-curdling scream he releases, the faces of the men in the room growing a few shades whiter with fear. Blood gushes from the spot his penis used to be, the appendage ripped from him by my claws. I smirk, backing away with my prize before using the claws of my left paw to start smashing the amputated penis into the ground. Had the men been quick enough, they could have saved it. But all four idiots stare at me in shock as I ground the small part into mince meat, almost resembling a pâté.

"Holly shit!" Someone exclaims quietly, the girls looking at me in awe with wide eyes. I nod to the girl that the now penis-less man had raped, seeing her mouth a quiet thank you to me as I back away from the ground meat and find a spot near the wall to lay against.

"She...she just...but...how?" Someone stammers unintelligibly as silence fills the room. I smile, letting my tongue loll out the side of my muzzle, thinking about the damage I can do if anyone else steps too close to me. The now penis-less man falls to the ground, curling into a ball as moans of agony fall from his lips.

"What the hell is going on in here?!" A shout sounds from a familiar-sounding voice. I shudder with anger and fear as a man comes into the cave, his face set into a scowl, and I recognize him as the one Caden and I fought earlier.

"Sorry, Beta Alsir." One of the men whimpers out, showing his neck in submission to this Alsir.

"It's just the she-wolf you brought back tore Mitch's dick off." He continues, waving in my direction. Alsir turns his beady gaze to me, chuckling as he turns to the man, Mitch, still on the ground, a puddle of blood slowly growing larger underneath him.

"I told you idiots not to go near or taunt her. It's Mitch's fault for not listening." Alsir sighs, his gaze returning to me.

"Someone take Mitch away from base and signal a medic crew. He won't be returning to the pack." With his order now said, Alsir leaves the cave and is most likely heading to somewhere beyond the only entrance and exit to this room. The two wolves standing by the entrance stare at each other for a quick moment before tentatively stepping towards me. They mean me no harm, and so I do not lunge at them. Besides, I need to come up with a plan to escape, and whether or not I will be taking the other she-wolves with me.

Watching the men as they draw closer to their fallen friend, a she-wolf with bright red hair catches my attention, her green eyes staring into my own. Her mouth moves as her hand points to the wolves growing closer to their friend, and it dawns on me what she is saying – blonde and key.

Turning my focus back to the two men, I realize that indeed one of them is blonde and attached to his belt loop is a ring of keys. I turn back to the redhead and nod, understanding what she is telling me. To get free, we need the keys the blonde wolf has. I am lucky that their focus is on Mitch, his agonizing scream as his two friends try to move him, giving me the perfect opportunity to climb to my paws and silently pad closer.

The room is silent as all the she-wolves watch in anticipation until I find myself once again at the end of my chain. With a silent sigh, I question the distance between me and the keys and note that if I swipe my paw, I can connect my claw to the ring and capture the first key to our escape.

With a quick swipe, I snarl, the men jumping in fright while letting out shrill screams of fear and backing away just in time for my claws to snatch the key ring away. I crouch low, covering my stolen items with my body as I continue to silently watch the men. They have Mitch held between them; their faces even paler from the fright I just gave the two. I smirk inwardly, happy to have gained something precious in freeing me from this place.

The men scurry away as fast as they can, Mitch letting out screams of pain that echo even as they leave the room. All that is left is the one male that is too busy making out with a she-wolf in the back corner to have noticed what we are doing.

Lying down, I turn to face the redhead as she sends me a questioning glance. With a wolfish grin and a nod, she sighs with relief as a hint of hope flashes in her eyes. The only thing left to do now is wait for the right opportunity to come.

Chapter 24 Caden

—————

Groaning from the pain coursing through my body, my eyes slowly open to the emptiness of the forest. Sunlight filters through the leaves, and I wonder just how long I have been out under the influence of the drug.

"Caden?!" A voice calls out my name, the words muffled as if my head is under water. Holding my hand to my pounding head, my eyes widen in shock. Some time between passing out from the drug to waking up, I must have shifted to my skin form.

"Caden?!" The voice calls again, this time louder. It seems whoever is looking for me is growing closer. Sitting up slowly, my ears pop, and the sounds of the forest come to life, clear as ever, making me wince. I was not ready for the immediate change in sound clarity. I wince, turning to see the dart still embedded in my skin and carefully pull it out. I thank the Goddess for my strong blood that allowed my body to metabolize the drugs quicker than a regular wolf.

"Caden!" My name is called out a third time, and I instantly recognize the voice just as the owner appears in front of me, pushing past a clump of bushes and looking around frantically.

"A-Amelia!" I call back, spotting the blonde she-wolf just before she sees me. With wide eyes of relief, Amelia rushes to my side as I stand, wrapping her arms around me and nearly knocking me off my feet while taking in my scent.

"Thank the Goddess I found you. When I woke up, you and Grace were gone!" She sobs out, her small body shaking. Guilt takes over as I pull her closer, letting Amelia cry her heart out. It was stupid of Grace and me to take on the Ragers and worry her. Stupid that Grace and I left her alone.

Grace!

Pulling away from Amelia, I turn frantically, trying to catch anything – a scent, a broken bush, any trail that would lead me to her.

"They...they took her." I whimper out, only able to catch the faint lingering of lavender and mint.

"W-what?" Turning to look at Amelia, her tear-streaked face now in a look of horror, I watch as she fights back a panic attack. The guilt grows inside me, knowing that I failed to protect the two she-wolves and keep them together. I watch as she begins sniffing the air, anxiety and fear radiating off of her in waves as she holds in her panic.

"I'm sorry. I tried to protect her, but they had a gun. A dart gun. That's why I was out of it." I state, pacing back and forth as I try to figure out where Grace might be. Relaying the map of The Run in my head over and over again, I try to figure out what cave might be large enough to hide the Ragers and their captives, but nothing comes to mind.

"She'll...she'll make it out. I know Grace, and she will come back to us." I hear her whisper. I think she is trying to convince herself though. Ragers are not ones to mess with, and sadly, we both knew Grace had a better chance at freedom if she killed herself. Once a Rager claims a she-wolf, she will never be free again.

"The ones that captured her said something about an Alpha. I have a feeling they won't do anything to her until their Alpha does." I voice out, thinking about the possibility of Grace still being unmated and finding a way to escape. Amelia turns to me with shock, a smile slowly forming on her face.

"Then she has a chance!" She states her eyes filling with hope for the first time since our reunion. I nod, taking a deep breath to calm my raging emotions. Amelia is right. If Grace is being saved for someone else, then there is still a fighting chance to find and rescue her.

"Caden here!" Amelia shouts, turning to see something being thrown at me and instantly catching my bag. I sigh, happy to know that Amelia had brought our stuff when she came searching for me and Grace and feeling the guilt once more. We should have never left her alone. Running my hand along the stubble that's grown on my face, I dig inside and grab a change of clothes, dressing quickly.

"How do we find her? Find Grace?" I ask, running my hand through my dirty hair and wincing from the pain in my shoulder where the one wolf bit me.

"I can mind link her. I know that mind links don't work much in this forest, but the closer we are, the stronger the link gets." Amelia suggests as I take Grace's pack from her. She carried three bags here already; the least I can do is lighten her load.

"As long as we can find her scent or the Ragers' scents, we can follow it to where she might be and hope that the link works." She continues, her blue eyes set in determination. It's a good plan – the only plan that may work really – but the problem is trying to find where the right trail is. I sigh, turning to stare at the spot I last saw the Ragers disappear in and question whether or not we can pull off a rescue mission. No wolf has ever taken a she-wolf from a Rager before, since their base within the Goddess' Forest is hidden.

"What if it doesn't work?" I ask quietly. Turning to look at Amelia.

"Then we pray she finds a way out herself, or she finds a way to kill herself."

Chapter 25 Grace

Time passed slowly while being chained to the wall, and Ragers came and went, raping a she-wolf for their own pleasure or seeing if they could taunt me into a reaction. My heart breaks when a she-wolf would scream in pain, their pleading and begging making it hard for me to stay still when all I want to do is come to their rescue. But I stay still. I have to protect the keys hidden under me that will unlock our freedom from here. If the Ragers find out I have them, then our only chance at escaping will be gone for good.

The redhead from before catches my attention once more, her eyes going from me to where the keys are hidden, her brow raised in a silent question – can we leave? I shake my head no, watching her eyes close in disappointment.

Unfortunately for us she-wolves, now is not the time to escape with men walking in and out. I have a feeling nightfall will be soon, and many of the Ragers who torture the poor women before will be falling asleep. With these wolves fast asleep and leaving hopefully the bare minimum to guard their base, we she-wolves will have to move during the night if we want a quick escape.

With a sigh, I rest my head on my paws, doing my best to conserve energy. I know the girls in here will be sore, barely able to move, and many will have to be helped, but nighttime will be our one and only shot at our freedom.

I do my best to drown out the she-wolves being raped, the scent of blood as they are forced to mate with the male using them lingering in the air. My eyes keep meeting the redhead, her determined gaze one that captivates me. She will make a great ally in our escape.

"Hey, it's nighttime time. We need to let the she-wolves rest." Sticking his head inside the room, Alsir calls out to the remaining men. I watch as the three in the middle of their activities groan in frustration, their bodies moving faster as they rush to finish their deed. I suppress the growl threatening to spill from my lips, wanting nothing more than to kill those few wolves who cause more pain to their victims.

"I said give them a rest!" Alsir growls out in warning, striding into the room and towards the one wolf who is forcing a she-wolf to gag on his dick. I watch as he pulls the wolf away, his clawed fingers slicing the male's erect penis right off. Blood splatters onto the she-wolf, her screams of terror ringing in the room.

"When I say let them rest, I mean let them rest. Someone take him and his dick out to medical aid. He won't be able to fuck anyone for a while until the medics reattach it to his body." Alsir orders the remaining two males to take their companion away from their Beta. No wonder Alsir had no remorse for Mitch after I tore his dick off; he does it as a punishment to the others.

Soon, all the Ragers file out of the cave, leaving us she-wolves alone. The redhead looks to me, her questioning gaze reminding me that now might be a good time to run. I nod my head, closing my eyes and allowing the shift to change my body from wolf to human. The drugs are not completely out of my system, and so the shift takes a few minutes longer than I'd like. Biting my lip from the pain, I listen as each bone bends and snaps into shape in case a Rager hears me shifting and comes to investigate.

Lucky for me, I soon find myself in my skin form with no issues. The chain rattles as I move, the collar around my neck loosening with my human form being smaller than my wolf. I carefully grab the keys from beside me, trying my best not to rattle the multitude of metal hanging together as I try to find the one that will unlock the collar on me. With ten attempts, I grin as the eleventh key fits snugly into the keyhole, and the satisfying click of the collar unlocking is heard.

I carefully take the collar off, settling it onto the ground before tiptoeing to the red head. Putting a finger to my lips, I quickly get to work finding the right key to take off her own collar, smiling triumphantly when the third key releases her.

"Keep silent and help me free the others," I whisper, the redhead nodding in response as we set off to the closest she-wolf. We work fast, her holding the collar while I search for the right key. When the lock unlocks, the redhead sets the collar down and motions for the freed she-wolf to wait for us by the exit. With quick work, the remaining twelve she-wolves are freed, and we are left with the next step of the plan – escaping.

The redhead and I join the others by the exit, some leaning on others in order to stay standing. It is clear that some of these wolves are Omegas, and if I hadn't been here, they would never have had a chance to escape.

"I have a feeling the Ragers won't be hunting for she-wolves as all the collars were in use. Right now, they should be asleep." I state in a whisper, making sure to keep my senses alert in case a Rager walks in.

"This is our chance to escape and make it out alive. Stay silent, stay vigilant, because no one will come back for you if any of the men here catch you." I warn, letting these girls know the harsh reality of the situation we are in. I look each one of them in the eyes, seeing a look of determination blazing in each girl, even if the scent of fear comes off of them, and smile. They are ready to fight.

"Let's go." I say firmly after making sure the thirteen she-wolves before me understand. As much as my words caused them fear, these ladies need to know the truth. If any one of them is caught, no one will be returning to save them. They will forever be stuck with their Rager mate, forced to bear pups and be raped by any and all males in the pack if they are not silent. With a nod to the she-wolves, I tiptoe to the door and stick my head out.

"I know the way out." I quiet voice whispers from my left. Turning, I find the redhead beside me.

"I woke up just in time for them to carry me from the entrance to their hideout. I can lead us out." She continues. I weigh her words and decide to trust her.

"Take the lead. I will take the rear." She nods at my order, slipping into the hall and padding towards the end where an intersection of the cave system meets. She looks around before nodding to me, and I send the she-wolves out after her.

Slowly and silently, each she-wolf tiptoes into the hall, their steps barely audible as they lean on their partner. I smile, the escape going smoother than I expected so far, as I am the last to leave the cave, leaving the keys locked in a collar and wondering if the Ragers will be able to free the keyring without the key to the collar grasped in my hand. My best bet is that they will need to replace all the collars come the next event.

I join the huddled girls at the end of the hallway, the redhead looking to me for a moment. I nod at her, motioning with my hand to lead the way as I keep an eye out for any Ragers. We are in the open, and at any moment, one can pop out and sound the alarm to their pack. The redhead stays just ahead of everyone, her head on a swivel as she too keeps her eyes and ears peeled for any movement not a part of the group, as the other girls follow her.

Thankfully, they stay silent as we are led down corridors of caves. The procession is agonizingly slow, but the hope building inside me has me believing that we will make it out of here alive and safe in no time.

Chapter 26 Caden

⸻

The sun beats down on Amelia and me as we continue walking deeper into the forest. Hours have passed since we started our search for Grace, and as we grow closer to the center where the lake sits, the less hope I have in finding her. With a defeated sigh, I lean against the nearest tree and take a deep breath.

"The good news is we are growing closer to the lodge." Amelia states sadly as she joins me in leaning against the tree, exhaustion clear as day in her blue eyes.

"The bad news is we can't find Grace." I add somberly, looking towards her. To think, just days ago, Amelia and I became friends looking for Grace in the first place, and now we are back to square one.

With a sad smile on my lips, I close my eyes and open my senses once more, trying to get any trace scent of Grace or the wolf that took her. I just want that hint of mint and lavender I have grown attached to, a strand of her silver fur glinting in the sunlight, giving me a clue on what direction she might have been taken in. Anything to find her and hold her tightly in my arms.

"Caden?" Amelia calls out softly, my eyes opening as I turn my attention to her.

"You're falling for her, aren't you?" She asks, her eyes soft with unshed tears as she takes my hand. I nod slowly, eyes widening as she brushes her fingers across my cheek, wiping away tears that I never realized had fallen.

"Then let's find her." She smiles encouragingly at me, pulling me away from the tree as we continue our search. My mind is whirling as I think of what I will do when I find Grace - find the she-wolf calling to my heart. Amelia is right, I have fallen for Grace, and after this stupid event is over, I plan to romance her until she is mine and I am hers. I just have to find her first.

"This is strange."

"Strange indeed."

"A male and a female, neither mated nor in love."

"What are they doing so close to the center?"

"Don't they know we lurk about?"

"They might, but something seems strange."

Three bell-like voices flitter about the forest, forcing Amelia and me to stop in our tracks. I had thought we had walked away from the Fae territory, but apparently I was wrong. With a growl of annoyance, I turn to Amelia, ready to warn her, but instead, I find her uncovering her ear with the earring on display.

"Oh, a token, she is a friend."

"I wonder if she is friends with Silver Fur."

"Oh, I love Silver Fur, she smells like lavender and mint."

"I wonder if Silver Fur is here in the forest."

Three small creatures appear before us, their wings fluttering fast yet silently as they circle Amelia. She smiles, holding her hand out flat as the one with blue wings lands gently on the palm of her hand.

"Hi, Sunny. I haven't seen you in forever." Amelia greets the pixie, a subspecies of the Fae.

"Melia, it's you!" Sunny smiles out with a giggle, her friends landing beside her.

"Yes, and we are actually looking for Silver Fur. Some Ragers took her." Amelia states. The pixies reel back in shock, their already large eyes growing larger as they huddle together.

"Are you sure they took Silver Fur?"

"She is a fighter, how could she be taken?"

"We are sure. I was there when they took her." I answer the pixies, stepping closer to Amelia to look each one of them in their eyes.

"The one that seems to be their Leader is the one that took her. He had a dart gun that knocked the two of us out." I continue, the pixies looking even more shocked.

"Those bastards. How could they do that to Silver Fur!" Sunny explodes in anger, stomping her little feet against Amelia's hand.

"Rain and Nova, go let the Princess know what is going on. I will guide Golden Boy and Melia to the Ragers." Sunny orders, the two pixies nodding in respect before taking off. Sunny smiles in satisfaction before her little wings begin to flutter, and she takes off.

"Follow me this way!" She calls out, leaving Amelia and me to have no choice but to follow her. Hopefully, with the help of these pixies, we will be able to save Grace in time.

Chapter 27 Grace

Holding my hand out to stop the girls from moving, I watch as a Rager walks past our hiding spot, his greasy blonde hair slicked back and his dirty clothes indicating he has just returned for the night. This wolf must have been on the night watch patrolling the area. The redhead and I look at each other, and she points to the right side – the side this Rager came from – and mouths *exit* to me. I grin, turning just in time to watch the Rage disappear into a doorway and slamming it shut, giving us a clear path to the exit.

"Now is our chance. Stay silent but move fast." I whisper to the other girls. Their nervousness floats in the air like a cloud, but they all nod happily, their eyes shining with the final stretch to freedom being so close. Counting down from three, I take a deep breath and pad into the hallway, keeping an eye on the room the Rager disappeared into while the redhead helps to guide the others to the exit.

Every second that ticks down, I pray to the Moon Goddess that no Ragers find us. It seems my prayers are answered as the last she-wolf disappears behind me, giving me the chance to fall back and join the others at the door. I smile, realizing we are so close to our freedom now - something no she-wolf has ever done after being captured by Ragers. This beats any bet I have with the Alpha of my pack.

"Before we open this door, I need to know how many of you were marked by a Rager." State, looking at the girls one by one. Six she-wolves raise their hands; their faces filled with shame. I smile gently at them, spying the fading mark on their neck.

"Good news is, if you or your mate was with another wolf right after the mark was placed, your mark will fade within twenty-four hours. You all will be mateless come tomorrow morning." My words seem to be the light of hope these girls needed as their shame turns to shock, and then happiness. It seems these are the words they needed to hear, as many she-wolves that are taken by Ragers are found either dead at the end of The Run, or never to be seen again.

"Now let's push this stupid door open and get the hell away from here." The redhead chuckles out, moving towards the heavy steel door blocking our final path to freedom. With a smile, I watch as she pushes against it, the door slowly moving forward. I move forward, joining her as we use what remaining strength we have to push our way out until a blinding light greets us.

Letting my eyes adjust to the change in lighting, I slowly walk out the door and onto soft sand. The sound of waves lapping out to us fills my ears, and as my vision finally clears, I stand in awe at the sight before us. Crystal blue waters surround the island we are on, and dread fills me. We are on crystal paw lake, the largest lake dead center in the forest. Legends say a monster lurks in these waters, and no wolf is ever found once they go for a swim.

"Are we where I think we are?" The redhead asks, and I nod, still coming to terms that we jumped out of one danger into another.

"It's just a legend, right? If we swim, we should be safe?" Another she-wolf asks.

"Shift to wolf form." I order, ignoring the question, motioning for the redhead to take the lead once more.

"It'll be easier to swim, and our fur will keep us warm. But swim fast and do not look back." I continue, the sounds of bones breaking following my words. I watch as wolves of all colours run into the water, each she-wolf swimming as fast as they can before I, too, shift and take the rear. Some she-wolves lag behind with their strength depleted from the endless rape they endured, but the others help support them when they falter, making me proud of their camaraderie as we swim with the setting sun behind us.

Halfway to the other side of the lake, the forest suddenly grows quiet, and unease settles into me. Something is wrong. I can feel it. Shifting back into my skin side mid swim, I gasp at the cold, icy water that laps against my skin and force myself to stay afloat. If I stay in this form, I will freeze to death within minutes. The others continue swimming, but I can see the red wolf, my companion who helped with the escape, looking at me with concern as she waits for me to continue swimming with the others.

'*What if a monster truly lurks in these waters?*' I think while my eyes search the crystal blue lake. Howls of fury from the island sounds, and a sigh of relief escapes me. I would rather deal with Ragers in the water than a legendary monster.

"Get to the forest and find the biggest tree. There should be a tree house there and hide until help comes or I do." I say loud enough for the girls to hear, their already swift swimming becomes faster as the fear they felt from these men fuels them forward into their escape. Ragers soon pour out from the exit to their base, their fury radiating off of them like waves of the lake and reaching me. They are mad that their precious broodmares have escaped.

I listen closely as they begin to dive into the lake, their clothes soon growing heavy from the water. Had they been smart, they would have removed their clothing and shifted to chase after us, but it seems anger has clouded these men's judgment, giving me a chance to fight. I know water combat like the back of my hand thanks to my days spent in Grandfather's pack by the Ocean. I will be able to beat them without a fight or escape if it becomes too much to handle. I just need to distract these men long enough to buy the others more time to escape.

The Ragers are close now, the first being ten feet in front of me. Turning to make sure the others have made it to safety, I smile as I see no trace of them. Shifting back to wolf form, I duck under the water and paddle smoothly towards the closest Rager. He turns around in confusion, most likely wondering where I disappeared to as my fur blends nicely with the water.

Using his confusion against him, I swim up just in time for my teeth to sink into his jugular as he turns to face me. Hearing his howl of pain as I tear his throat open and swim away, I watch his final breath leave his body before he sinks into the water, and his blood dyes the crystal-clear water red. Hopefully, none of the coordinators saw me kill him, or else I will face some serious consequences. But, being as it was a Rager, I have a feeling they will turn a blind eye with their job being done for them.

Something shimmering under the surface of the water catches my attention, but I chalk it up to fish scales as I turn back to watch the other Ragers swim towards me with newfound fury. They had just watched me kill their packmate and were now out for revenge. Swimming to my right and away from the shores the she-wolves disappeared to, I led the Ragers on a wild goose chase, taking out any that managed to get too close to me.

Splotches of red now litter the crystal surface as five Ragers pursue me, but I am growing tired and weak. Being in the cold lake has taken its toll on me, and I will need to lose these five wolves soon if I want to survive. Turning my head to see the Ragers focusing on me, the shimmering I saw under the water earlier returns, catching my attention once more. Waves are being made where the shimmer appears, and fear creeps inside me. There are no winds tonight that are able to create waves as big as the ones behind the men, meaning the Ragers and I weren't alone in this lake.

My momentary distraction is my downfall as a Rager clamped his jaw around the scruff of my neck, digging in deeper than necessary as I feel his canines puncture my skin and the metallic smell of my blood reaches my nose. The water began to turn a pinkish hue from the blood trickling out of me, but this is the least of my concerns.

Cries of pain and fear sound behind this Rager and me, and we watch as wolves disappear into the crystal depths, never to return to the surface. The fear coursing through my body grows stronger, making me panic. I fight against the Rager that is holding me captive, recognizing him as Alsir by his scent. His teeth hold firm, and I howl and bark at him frantically trying to get this wolf to notice the urgency in my barks, but Alsir ignores me.

Suddenly, the water stills and a silence spreads along the lake. Alsir stops swimming, letting go of me. He and I can both sense the imminent danger lurking in the deep lake waters as I flail to regain buoyancy from his unexpected release of me, and he growls at the unknown. It is coming for us – whatever it is.

Then, the water's surface ripples and scales emerge glittering in the light. A massive tail like a mermaid's is the first thing I see as it propels whatever beast it belongs to towards us. I turn towards the shore, doing my best to swim away as Alsir does the same, an unspoken truce between us as we fight to survive. I am ahead of him, my speed unmatchable, with fear coursing through me, but I have the dumb idea to look back just as large jagged teeth appear behind Alsir and me.

Chapter 28 Caden

―――

"**R**agers made a base years ago in the lake." Sunny's cheery voice rings out beside my ear, the little pixie having grown tired of flying now sits on my shoulder.

"How did they manage that?" I ask, keeping to the path she had pointed out to us. We have been walking for twenty minutes since meeting the three pixies, Sunny, Amelia, and me, focused on saving Grace – Silver Fur as Sunny calls her. The little creature has been sharing stories of how she and her troupe have travelled the world, always returning to the Goddess's forest during The Run to gather magic under the full blue moon. I also learned how she and her friends came to know Grace and Amelia through Ocean Heart, Grace's Maternal family's pack, and how Grace has saved the Fae Princess on more than one occasion growing up. I think at this point, I am no longer shocked by just how incredible Grace is and instead, the urge to take her on a date and slowly fall in love with her has grown.

"No one knows. The Guardian of the lake never bothers them, as they usually use boats to travel. But even it has been growing irritated by the lack of respect the Ragers have." Sunny answers, kicking her little feet happily against my shoulder. I chuckle, her movements tickling me. I think when I take over, I will be making a garden in my pack for her and her troupe to visit whenever they want. It will be nice to have the pixies fly around and become allies with. But worry gnaws at me as I take in what she said about the Guardian of the lake. Legends have been told about a lake monster here in the forest, and many took it as a story. If Sunny says there is something in the lake, then Grace might be in greater danger.

The sound of twigs snapping just in front of us has Amelia and me stopping mid-step, our eyes finding one another before we prepare to fight whatever is coming our way. Without warning, a red she-wolf runs into me, causing me to fall onto my ass and Sunny to take flight in order not to be smooshed.

"Hey, hey. I am not going to hurt you!" I say softly, seeing the she-wolf standing over me with lips pulled back into a snarl. I stay where I am, looking to Amelia, who sighs and slowly walks over.

"He won't hurt you. He and I are looking for a friend of ours." She states, placing a gentle hand on the wolf's shoulder. She gently smooths her fur, doing her best to calm the red wolf down. Others soon join us in the small path, a total of what I can see being thirteen she-wolves, and I wonder just where they came from, as some look like they have been through hell with their damp fur and exhaustion behind their eyes.

The sound of shifting brings my attention back to the red she-wolf looming over me until a petite redhead stands beside Amelia.

"Are you friends with the silver-haired she-wolf?" The redhead asks, catching my attention instantly. Amelia nods as I stand, the need to find Grace growing stronger.

"She is still at the lake fighting the Ragers." She continues, a small smile on her lips.

"She saved all of us, so please, go save -" I don't stick around to hear the rest of her words, my legs already racing down the path towards the lake. If the she-wolves escaped because of Grace, then she must be close, must be alive.

Crashing through the last of the shrubbery, I find myself on the sandy shores of the lake, the crystal blue waters dyed red in many places. Something happened here, something so big that it killed many wolves.

"Grace?!" I shout out, cupping my hands around my mouth as I frantically search the shores. I can smell her, smell her blood. She is injured and in need of help. Her scent of lavender and mint permeates the air, causing the fear and anxiety inside me to grow.

"Grace?!" I call out again, tripping over a buried log in the sand and cursing my racing mind. I need to calm down if I am to find her.

"Grace!" I am losing hope, my heart breaking as I stand once more. What if she had died, and I will never see her again? What if I am too late and the Ragers have taken her to a new base? What if -

"Caden?" I freeze, the scent of lavender and mint filling my nose as the soft voice of the woman I have been searching for calls out to me, cutting off my train of thought. I turn to the right, Grace lying on the shore, her battered body half out of the cold water. Without a second thought, I find myself racing to her side, kneeling onto the soft sand, and pulling her body close

"You're okay." I whisper out while tears flow down my cheeks. I was never more relieved in my life to have her in my arms than I am now. How her soft body fits against mine and knowing that she is alive - that she is safe - is the best feeling I have ever felt.

Chapter 29 Grace

———

Frozen in terror, I watch as the sharp teeth from the lake monster draw near. Alsir is no match for it as he disappears into its mouth, the monster diving down into the depths of the lake. I use this chance to start swimming again, as the water where Alsir once was soon grows red with his blood. The cold water laps against my fur, weighing me down, and I realize that if I want to get away faster, I will need to shift. Diving under the water, I allow my body to make the painful shift to human before surfacing, using this chance to see if I can spot the monster. Sadly, I can see nothing before I surface, gasping for air before quickly resuming my escape from the monster that lurks in the depths of these normally calm waters.

"Do not be afraid." A whimsical voice fills my ears, the gentle tone of the words slowing me down as I wonder where this voice comes from. Turning around, I look back to where Alsir once was, questioning if I imagined the voice. Turning back, my body freezes as I come face-to-face with the lake beast. Before me is a gorgeous water dragon with glimmering scales, her head held at my level as her body sinks deep into the water. Blue eyes as clear as the water stare warmly at me, the predatory gaze I felt earlier now gone as she gently breathes in and out, leaving soft ruffles of waves on the surface.

For a moment, I forget to stay afloat, the shock and fear paralyzing me as I begin to sink. A soft surface pushes from under me back up from the water, and I cough the small amount of liquid I ended up swallowing.

"I won't hurt you, little wolf." The voice continues, the dragon tilting her head as she smiles gently at me, her green and blue-scaled body floating on the water – a body I find myself kneeling on.

"Then...then why did you hurt the Ragers?" I ask, weary of this creature.

"I have been waiting for a reason to kill those males, and you gave that reason to me. Thank you, Silver Wolf." She chuckles out, her clear blue eyes giving me the feeling of a mother looking at her child. All fear I have for this creature vanishes as she bows to me, her body lowering me into the water gently. She waits for me to swim a few feet away, giving me one last friendly smile before diving back into the depths of the lake. Her swift movements unfortunately send a large wave crashing into me before I can get my bearings, sending me under the water once more as I fight against the strong current. I feel my back connecting with a rock, the little air I have left rushing out of my lungs and allowing water to enter instead. My vision becomes hazy, the water and darkness becoming a comfort to me as my eyes slowly close.

The sounds of waves crashing against the shore bring my groggy mind back to reality as my body starts to shake. I cough, the lake water that I swallowed quickly spilling from my lip until I am finally able to take a gasp of breath. My beaten and battered body refuses to move, and I lie helplessly on the sandy shore, the waves lapping at my body. The last thing I remember is drowning, so how did I end up safe on the other side?

[Sorry about the unintentional wave, Silver Wolf. I did not mean to harm you.] The whimsical voice of the dragon floats in my mind. I do not question how she is able to mind link me, as dragons are mystical creatures, their powers on par with the goddess. I send a silent thank you, knowing she saved my life after nearly drowning me.

Closing my eyes in exhaustion after the events I have just been through, I wonder if I will win the bet on a technicality of dying, if my last moments will be spent lying by the lake without being able to see Amelia or Caden again.

"Grace?!" My name reaches my ears. It is faint, almost as if carried on the wind. I smile, thinking it is my time to go, and someone on the moon is calling to me.

"Grace?!" The voice is nearer, a deep male voice that calls my name, the owner sounding frantic and hopeful. One thing is for sure, this voice is not coming from the sky, but from near the forest. Maybe someone has come to save me, but they are too far away to know who the voice belongs to.

"Grace!" The voice is close now, and my eyes open as tears fill my eyes as I recognize the voice, my heart pounding as I try to find the strength to call out to him. He found me. He really came and found me.

"Caden?" I call out as soon as I find the strength, my voice weak and croaky from the coughing and the lake water I ingested. For a moment, I am unsure if he heard me, unsure if I truly heard him or if my imagination is playing tricks on me. And then I smell him. His scent of fresh forest on a winter's day mixed with anxiety and relief. Strong arms gently cradle me from the sand as I am wrapped in Caden's embrace, the feeling of being safe washing over me.

"You're okay." He whispers out, his tears falling from his eyes and onto my cheek. I smile, slowly reaching up to brush away his tears with shaking fingers as my whole body relaxes into his touch. I am safe with him, secured in his arms, knowing he will take me away from this god-awful place.

"I'm sorry." He sobs out, pressing his forehead against mine and breathing in my scent.

"I let them take you. I will never let it happen again." He continues, placing a soft kiss on my forehead. I smile, my heart skipping a beat at the gentleness. No wolf has ever been this gentle to me. They always treated me like an object to claim or an obstacle to train. But here is Caden, holding me, kissing me and allowing himself to be vulnerable with me.

"You didn't let them take me." I croak out, my voice still hoarse.

"They took me as you fought, and then you came to rescue me." My voice cracks as my tears spill, this overwhelming feeling of hope and love filling my heart. Suddenly, without a warning, his lips are pressed to mine, moving gently as he swallows whatever else I wanted to say.

My eyes slowly close, and a small moan escapes my throat when his teeth nip my bottom lip. I find myself kissing him back, my lips moving in sync with his as he pulls my body closer to his. His tongue darts across my closed lips, seeking permission to enter, and I agree, parting my lips just enough for our tongues to tangle with one another.

Another moan escapes me, my heart beating faster and my shivering body feeling warmer by the second. And just as suddenly as it began, the kiss ends, and we find ourselves panting for breath with our foreheads pressed together once more.

"When The Run is over and we are safely out of this forest, will you go on a date with me?" I ask, my face feeling hot and flustered as I stare into his emerald green eyes.

"Couldn't you at least let me be the stereotypical guy and ask you out first?" He jokingly asks, his lips that were just on mine set into a carefree grin. I giggle, feeling the absurdity of the situation. I came to The Run set on winning a bet and freeing my pack members from being forced to come here. Now I am looking at a man I have slowly grown feelings for, who I hope to continue to get to know.

"Nope, I'm the boss." I state, getting a kiss on the forehead from him in response.

"Fine, you are the boss, Grace. But I get to plan the date." He whispers, tucking a strand of my wet hair behind my ear, the feeling of a thousand butterflies fluttering in my stomach, making me blush.

"Do I want to know why the two of you are cuddling by the water's edge, or have you already marked and mated her, Caden?" Amelia's voice sounds from my left, making Caden and me jump. I wince, the pain in my back reminding me of the injury I received slamming into the rock, and I suppress a whimper of pain.

"Shit! You okay, Grace?" Amelia asks, her joking tone gone as she comes to kneel beside Caden and me.

"Just a small injury, nothing some rest can't fix." I answer, happy to be reunited with my best friend.

"Why don't you come rest at our camp then!" A voice chimes out; one I recognize easily. A little pixie with blue butterfly-like wings flutters towards me, landing on Caden's shoulder as her large eyes look at me in concern.

"Hi, Silver Fur." Sunny chimes in, giving me a soft smile.

"Hi, Sunny. If you can promise that my friends and I can leave safely, then I would love to rest at your camp." I yawn out, already having a feeling that the Princess has sent this offer for the small pixie to extend.

"Princess Airia already sent a messenger. You, Melia and Cade are welcome to rest with us." Sunny agrees, her face lighting up with a smile.

"Then lead the way, Sunny. Grace has been through a lot, and she needs her rest." Caden states before I can answer, placing another soft kiss on my forehead. The pixie takes flight, landing on Amelia's shoulder this time as she happily chats away with the blonde wolf. I smile, Caden carefully positioning my body so that my head rests on his shoulder before he stands with me in his arms. The lakeside is quiet, and I think back to the dragon, wondering if I will ever meet her again. Looking over Caden's shoulder, his steady heartbeat lulls me to sleep, and the last thing I see is the tail of the dragon waving at me before she vanishes into the deep waters.

Chapter 30 Caden

———

I watch as the Faeries work on Grace, covering her body in healing lotions and tonics. Sunny had led us through the forest for an hour, the path taking us closer towards the lodge before we came to a cave hidden by vines. After another twenty minutes of walking through the cave, we emerged into a valley with a large opening in the sky and were greeted by the Faerie Princess Airia. Her pointed ears and moon white skin stood out amongst the growing flowers and colourful crystals deep in the hidden valley.

When she saw the injured Grace in my arms, her first instinct was to rush Grace and me into a room carved out of the stone walls where maids had us bathe in separate pools, the maids leaving me alone as they cared for the injured wolf. As soon as she was cleaned, the maids whisked Grace away to be treated without informing me. I nearly went crazy when I realized Grace was missing again and would have caused a war if Sunny hadn't appeared when she did, telling me to follow her to see Grace.

Now I sit in a soft chair, donning a Fae silk robe, my eyes never leaving Grace's sleeping face. Her silver hair has been washed clean; the strands braided out of the way into a side fishtail braid. Her maids make sure to keep their movements light and gentle as they massage the cream into her skin. With each movement their hands make, I watch as some of the bruises slowly fade away, and relief fills me. Grace will be fine.

"She is brave, our Silver Fur." A musical voice calls out, Princess Airia coming into the room.

"She is also loyal and deserves the same loyalty and truth, Caden." The Princess continues, running a hand through her cyan hair as her teal eyes look at me with a glare.

"You know who I am, Airia. It isn't the first time we met." I sigh out, glaring back at the Fae.

"This is true. But Grace doesn't know." She counters back, her eyes glinting in the dim light. She is right, though. Grace doesn't know the full truth of who I am.

"Don't waste this chance at love by keeping secrets." With that, the Princess leaves, and the maids soon follow, leaving only Grace and me in the room. I watch the slow rise and fall of her chest as she sleeps, her face so calm and peaceful. She's been through hell these last few hours, and I can only imagine what those Ragers did when she was in her grasp or if she ran into the Guardian of the lake in her escape. Footsteps approach the room, and I turn to see Amelia enter, her gaze landing on me for a brief moment before leaning against the doorway as her blue eyes watch her friend.

"So." Amelia states after a few moments of awkward silence pass between us

"You and Grace?" She quickly adds as I turn to face the blonde with a small smile. I can tell by the protective tone in her words that this will be a long conversation.

"There is no me and Grace. Not yet anyway." I answer carefully, not knowing what else to say.

"She wants to date me after The Run, and I want to make her mine." I continue, looking back to the sleeping girl who now has a soft smile on her face.

'Grace must be having some really nice dreams.' I think, happy to see her finally getting some peaceful sleep.

"Good, because if you think you're going to mate her right away, you're wrong. I will kill you if you even-"

"Amelia." I cut her off, holding a finger to my lips as her voice slowly grows louder, and a frown appeared on Grace's face, and she fidgets as her dreams are interrupted. Amelia looks away sheepishly, guilt visible on her as Grace settles down and her frown disappears. Sending a sharp look to Amelia, I make sure that Grace is asleep before continuing our conversation.

"I have been alone with the two of you on more than one occasion. You know I am not that kind of man." I state quietly, a little hurt from the distrust after everything we have been through the last few days. But I also understand where Amelia is coming from. She and Grace are inseparable, chosen sisters as they have put it. I still remember how Grace's wolf felt standing above me, snarling because she thought I was a threat to Amelia just days ago.

"Caden...I'm..." Amelia stutters out, guilt laced in her voice, and I smile as she tries to apologize. I know Amelia means no harm; she is just protective of her sister.

"Look, I told you I wanted to be with someone I love when we first met." I point out, getting a small nod in response from the blonde wolf.

"I mean it. I want to date Grace and get to know her more. She deserves a man who will love and protect her, and I plan to be that man." I finish, standing from my chair and walking to Amelia. Reaching out, I pull her into my arms for a hug and rest my chin on top of her head.

"I'm sorry, Caden." Amelia's voice is small as she returns my hug, her own sigh escaping from her lips.

"Don't worry, I understand how protective you are of her, and it's the same way she feels about you. You two are sisters, whether you share the same blood or not. I just hope you can give us your blessing." I reassure her, getting a giggle from Amelia.

"You already have it. Just promise me you will make her happy." She replies softly.

"I promise you I will do everything to make Grace happy and be a man she can rely on." I promise her, letting Amelia pull away from me and watching her walk to Grace's bedside. She plants a soft kiss on Grace's cheek, whispers something into her ear and walks back towards me.

"Get some sleep, Caden. She won't be waking up till tomorrow morning." She smiles, placing a hand on my shoulder.

"I will. Good night, Amelia."

"Good night, Caden." Amelia turns to look at Grace one last time before leaving the room. She must have been assigned her own room while I was taking care of Grace with the Fae maids, and knowing Amelia, as soon as her head hits the mattress, she will be knocked out.

Once again, it is just Grace and me in the room, her scent reaching me, tantalizing me. I have grown to love this scent – crave smelling it – and now with Grace agreeing to a date, I can become addicted to it. With a smile, I make my way towards the bed, debating on whether or not to climb in and pull Grace into my arms or return to my room. In the end, against my better judgment, I climb into the bed and carefully wrap my arms around the sleeping girl I have grown feelings for. I watch her sleep, breathing in her scent and listening to the steady beating of her heart.

The last thought running through my mind as sleep takes over is that I can get used to sleeping beside her.

Chapter 31 Grace

―――

Warmth.

That is what surrounds me.

The feeling of a solid body against mine as I lie on a comfortable surface that smells like sunlight on a summer day calms me, making me feel safe and secure. I smile, snuggling closer to the warm body and am happy to not feel any pain or exhaustion anymore.

"Is she up yet?" Someone whispers, their lyrical voice reaching my ears.

"Not yet. But I think she will be soon." Caden's voice answers back, fingers lighting running down my back. His scent wraps around me, relaxing my mind and body and making me feel safer than I have in days. With a soft sigh, I decide to see exactly where we are and slowly open my eyes to see a well-defined collar bone, one I want to sink my teeth into and claim as mine.

"Good morning, Lady Silver." Caden chuckles, his fingers grazing my cheek softly.

"G...good morning." I mumble back sheepishly, looking up to see Caden gazing at me, a soft and gentle smile on his lips.

"Good morning, Silver Fur. Glad to see you awake." The lyrical voice from before chimes in from the corner, piquing my curiosity about who it could be. Only the Fae call me Silver Fur, a nickname they have given me since my first shift. Which means this voice belongs to someone I know. Frowning, I try my best to sit up, only to feel Caden move away for a moment to assist me until I am comfortably leaning against the headboard of the bed.

"Oh, Airia, it's you!" Shocked by the presence of the Faerie Princess, I smile at my old friend as she sips from her teacup, a smirk on her light pink lips.

"Yes, it's me. And it seems you still refuse to use formalities." Airia chuckles out in amusement, placing her cup on the side table before standing and making her way to my side of the bed. With a smile, she sits beside me, her slim hand taking my left one before closing her eyes.

"You were severely injured on your back as well as on the brink of death through exhaustion." She states, her magic slowly seeping into my fingertips and mixing with my own. I feel some strength return to me; my eyes closing from the warmth her magic brings.

"Luckily for you, your friends came across Sunny. Had anyone else come across her, you would never have been found and would have died." The Faerie continues, patting the top of my hand. I open my eyes to see her staring at me with a sad smile, worry displayed in the depths of her eyes.

"Why is it I always find you injured?" She chuckles out, making me look down in guilt.

"Because no one looks out for me most days." I answer out, thinking back to the many times Airia and I have come into contact since our first introduction ten years ago. The first time was when she and her entourage lived in the forest by Silver Birch for a summer. This was just after a doctor saved me and reunited me with my grandfather's pack. I had been beaten by my father the moment I came back from Ocean Heart. He was furious when I walked in on him with a she-wolf interrupting their time together. I somehow managed to escape and hide in the forest where Airia and her people found me.

I spent a few days there with them, healing and learned from the Fae that I had some sort of power that allowed me to see into the forest. Powers that, with the help of the Fae training, I learned to control and grow my own strength.

"Well, that seems not to be the case anymore with Caden here. Keep my Silver Fur safe or else Golden Wolf." Airia sighs, directing her threat to the man holding onto me.

"I will try my best." Caden states solemnly, placing a kiss on my forehead. I feel my cheeks growing warm and duck my head so that the others don't see the raging blush growing along my face.

"Grace! You're awake!" Amelia's voice sounds from the doorway, her excitement and relief hitting me like waves as my friend rushes to the bed and joins the three of us already on there. She takes my free hand and holds it close to her, her blue eyes looking into mine as she searches my face.

"How do you feel?" She asks, taking a deep breath and breathing in my scent.

"Better, but still slightly sore." I answer honestly, giving Amelia a reassuring smile.

"Good. You have been out of it all night. Today is the fifth day!" She sighs out, her lips forming a tight grim smile as she looks down at our hands.

"What?!" In disbelief, I look up to see Caden and Amelia looking away guiltily as if this information wasn't supposed to be told to me.

"Melia and Caden brought you here last night. You currently have two more nights to reach the lodge." Airia says grimly, pulling my attention to her.

"Then we need to leave and make a break for it!" I practically yell, taking my hands from Amelia and Airia and trying to wiggle free from the bed. Strong arms pull me close, and I find myself nestled once more in Caden's embrace.

"Grace, we know winning the bet means a lot to you, but you were seriously injured. You could have died!" His voice is low and soothing, pausing any movement I may have had as he keeps me still. I can feel my sore body agreeing to his words, knowing full well that I did, in fact, nearly drown. But at the same time, I have a bet to win. One that will bring about a better future for Silver Birch.

"I know that Caden. But I can't just sit here and hide away." I growl in frustration. He sighs, the tips of his fingers coming to lift my chin so that our eyes meet.

"Fine. We will continue The Run on one condition." He states, his emerald eyes telling me that either I agree to this condition or we are stuck with the Fae for the remainder of The Run.

"And what condition is that?" I ask, afraid to know the answer.

"You ride on my back until you are healed."

Chapter 32 Caden

———

Watching Grace say goodbye to the Fae has a smile growing on my face. Apparently, Princess Airia and Grace are close friends, closer than I thought initially, and seeing how the Fae Princess kept my secret safe has me rethinking when I should tell Grace the truth of who I am.

Waiting with Amelia and Sunny, who sits on Amelia's head, I think about what I need to do when I make it to the lodge. Zander has already gathered wolves that support me, and the plan to take my rightful place has been set in motion. I will need to be fast as well if it means stopping Felix from being named Heir. But most importantly, I will need to keep the two she-wolves I have travelled with safe from my father and cousin. Goddess knows that those power-hungry men will try anything to have either of these strong women.

"Sorry about that." Grace sheepishly apologizes as she makes her way towards me, a backpack fixed to her back. Her dirty clothes have been changed into a slick pair of black leggings and a black fitted hoodie; her silver hair tied back into a braid. We all felt better with the baths from last night, the hospitality shown to us by the Fae being something I will not forget and will return tenfold when I take over my father's position.

Wagging my tail, I stand and trot towards the woman who has captured my heart, nuzzling Grace's cheek. She giggles as my fur tickles her, my tail swaying happily, knowing that her attention is on me.

"Well, I will be your guide out of the Fae camp." Sunny excitedly states, her wide eyes holding a sense of adventure, her little blue wings folded neatly behind her back

"We are taking a different route than how we got here, and where we exit will be about a day's run to the lodge." The pixie continues. I nod my head, ready to leave so as not to miss our chance at Grace winning the bet. With any luck, tomorrow night we will be safe and sound in the lodge. Grace scratches behind my ear, distracting me momentarily as I lean into her touch and pant happily, my tongue lolling out the side. She laughs, giving me a look of amusement before turning to Sunny.

"I guess we should be going now. Airia packed this bag with food for us so we will be good to go all night." Grace states, her hand leaving my ear as she moves to my side, making me miss her touch instantly. I bend down, allowing her to climb onto my back and relish in the feel of her weight on me while she stretches out. Her hands come around my neck, and her fingers interlock to keep her from falling off.

Grace settles with a small contented sigh before she lets me know she is ready, and we take off. I allow Amelia to take the lead with Sunny on her head, the little Pixie telling the blonde wolf when to turn in the maze-like walls of trees that the Fae have created to protect their camp. We have no fear of bumping into mateless wolves now, nor Ragers, as Grace explained earlier this morning that the Guardian of the lake wiped them out. This was good news for all of us. It meant the next event, the Ragers won't be participating in The Run. Now all we need to do is follow Sunny's direction and keep a steady pace to make it safely to the lodge.

It takes most of the day and hours of us running through the maze with a small break to eat the food packed for us, before the trip comes to an end. By now, the sun had set hours ago, and we find ourselves in front of a large weeping willow tree. Its long branches sway in the wind as it sits beside a small pond surrounded by a meadow of wild flowers shrouded in the blue glow of the moon. The scene is calming, a perfect place for a picnic date. But now is not the time for romance. We only have another day to run and make it to the lodge.

"This is where we part." Sunny mutters sadly, her big eyes filled with unshed tears. Grace sits up, her legs squeezing slightly to keep herself from falling off me as she holds out her palm. Taking the chance, Sunny places a soft kiss on Amelia's head before flying over to us and landing on the offered palm.

"Thank you for guiding us, Sunny. When this is all over, come visit me, okay!" Grace states, her voice light and cheery.

"I will, Silver Fur. Stay safe." With that, we watch the pixie fly back into the maze entrance, watching as the branches of the trees bend and weave with each other until a wall of wood and leaves remains where the maze opening once was.

Shocked, I stare at the greenery for a moment before Grace reminds us we need to leave, and leave we do. We have until tomorrow at midnight to make it to the Lodge for Grace to win the bet. Grace leans against my back once more, hooking her arms around me and letting me know I can take off. With the night still going strong, we race in the direction of the Lodge.

The forest is quiet; many wolves are either already safely at the Lodge or curled in a cave, mated to another wolf. Maybe a few stragglers still rushing to get to the Lodge un-mated remain, but they will be too focused on either securing a mate or fighting off the desperate males.

"Leave us alone!" A shout to our left sounds. I pause, my front right paw in the air as I look in the direction of the shout. Grace shifts above me, taking a deep breath, and I silently curse. The wind blows in our direction, bringing the scent of at least three wolves and the iron tang of blood. Someone is in danger, and I recognize at least one of the scents.

"I will not hand my mate over!" The same voice shouts in anger. It seems some wolves are truly desperate and will stop at nothing to claim a mate. Grace shifts again, her body leaning towards the direction the voice came from. With a sigh, I carefully step to the left, feeling Grace lean back onto my body as Amelia trails after me. I have a feeling tonight will be a long night.

The sounds of a fight coming to an end can be heard as we grow closer, and anger grows inside me. Pushing past some bushes, I come face to face of a man trying to crawl his way towards another who has positioned himself between the legs of an unconscious female. The fur along my spine bristled as

I let out a low warning growl, recognizing this wolf as Leon – a guard under my father. I watch as all movement stops, Leon visibly stiffening with fear as his head slowly moves towards me.

"A...Alpha. I see you found a m-mate." Leon stutters out, slowly standing and backing away from the she-wolf. His hand moves to cover his erect penis, and I growl again, already feeling anger rising in me. To think I would run into him here.

[Leave now.] I command, allowing the power in my blood to seep into my words. Leon nods, his fear keeping him mute as she shifts into his muddy brown wolf, and he runs away towards the direction of the Lodge with his tail between his legs.

I feel Grace stiffen above me; her eyes trained on the muddy brown wolf, and anxiety replaces the anger inside me when she slides off of me, rushing to the injured male and helping him to stand. Amelia pauses her steps, her blue eyes looking at Grace with concern before moving to guard the she-wolf. I pad over to Grace and the man, Grace giving me a somewhat cold look as I let the man lean against me instead to help alleviate his weight from Grace's shoulders. The man throws his arm around me, his fingers gripping my fur with each step we take until we reach the she-wolf, where he promptly kneels beside her, pulling her into his arms.

"Thank you so much for saving us." He whimpers out, his green eyes filling with tears. Grace takes out some medicinal tonics that Princess Airia gave us, helping the man feed them to his mate before she gives me a glare I haven't seen since we first met.

"I want answers Caden."

Chapter 33 Grace

———

I watch as Caden shifts, his fur receding into his body as the bones realign themselves. Guilt is present in his posture as he stands before me in his human form, his emerald-green eyes not meeting my gaze. I had seen the tattoo on the wolf that called him Alpha, a tattoo only belonging to the wolves that guard the Alpha King.

"Caden, who was that?" I ask, my arms hugging my body as I try to keep the hurt I feel from showing. Caden is someone from the Royal pack, a pack that caused this Goddess forsaken event hundreds of years ago.

"A pack mate of mine." He answers, honesty radiating from his body. I stiffen, realizing the hidden meaning in his words. If that wolf is Caden's pack mate, then that means Caden is indeed from the Royal pack, and I have a feeling of who his true identity is.

"Who are you?" I ask in a whisper, my eyes closing as I try to calm my frantic heart and give the man before me a chance to tell me the truth.

"I can't tell you. It's the one thing that I have to keep from you to protect you." He counters frantically, his words sounding like a plea for me to understand.

"Who are you?" I ask again, this time allowing the anger and hurt in me to surface.

"I can't tell you. I'm sorry." He whimpers out. I open my eyes to find him staring at me, his eyes filled with regret and...fear. Fear of what, I do not know, and right now I am too hurt to care. I turn away from him, not wanting Caden to see the tears gathering in my eyes. In such a short amount of time, he has found his way into my heart and knowing he has kept something from me hurts. Strong arms wrap around me from behind, pulling me against a sturdy chest as his scent surrounds me.

"I can't tell you everything. Not until The Run is over and plans that have been set are in motion." His words are low, his lips just beside my ear as he speaks. I allow my senses to open, to sniff out any lie he may try to hide. But his words are the truth and ease the tension inside my heart.

"But I can tell you that my name is Caden and that I am from Wœlf Haven in a sense. It is my mother's pack and I trained there." Caden continues, his heart beating calmly against my back from inside his chest. Another set of truths. He isn't lying to me, at least.

"And I promise that everything I have told you from meeting you to now is the truth. So please, just be patient and wait till we get to the Lodge for me to tell you everything." I take a deep breath, silence stretching between us. I can sense Amelia trying to link me, her wolf form pacing back and forth as the tense air between Caden and me grows.

[Grace?] She asks, pushing through the block I had tried to maintain between us, not wanting my best friend to see the turmoil in my mind.

"Why should I trust you?" I ask, allowing Caden to gently turn my body to face him and allow him to see the tears that have spilled down my cheeks. He carefully wipes them away, a soft and gentle smile on his face as he holds me close.

"Because I haven't lied to you, but I haven't told you everything about me." He whispers, his own eyes filled with tears as he places a kiss on my forehead. Closing my eyes, I think about his words and decide whether or not I should accept the answers he has given. He kept his identity from me for a reason.

[Grace, what do we do?] Amelia asks, her snout nudging my arm as she lets out a soft whimper. I feel Caden stiffen, but he doesn't release me and waits for me to say something.

[We get to the lodge and let him explain] I answer back, hearing a sigh of relief coming from my friend. She knows how I feel about someone betraying me, about how easily my trust can be broken. And right now, I feel like the trust I had in Caden has been shattered into a million shards.

[Will we leave him if he tries anything on our last leg of The Run?] Amelia questions, her words causing me to stiffen this time. Not once has Caden tried anything towards us, but that isn't to say now he might try a last-ditch effort in keeping me beside him. But deep down, I know Caden is a man of his word. If he says he will tell me everything at the Lodge, then he will tell me everything at the Lodge.

[No. Caden already knows he is on a rocky path with me. We won't leave until we get answers.] This seems to relieve Amelia as she makes a sound of agreement before our link is closed. Caden holds me closer to him, his chin resting on top of my head as we allow silence to settle between us.

Suddenly, a gasp is heard from where we left the male and his mate, making me turn around to see the she-wolf sitting up and looking around dazed. Leaving Caden's side, I jog over to the she-wolf and kneel beside her, taking a deep breath to see if I can find anything in her scent that might indicate there is any other injury.

"What happened?" She asks dazed, her confused expression taking in the area around us.

"You were unconscious because of another male. But you're safe now." I answer, Amelia bringing the bag over to me. I rummage through and find some buns the Fae packed, handing one each to the wolves before me and watch as they scarf the food down. It seems they haven't eaten in a while.

"These people scared off that wolf. Apparently, that man over there is his Alpha." The male states, nodding his head towards Caden, who now wears a pair of shorts. He must have taken them from the bag before Amelia brought it to me.

"You saved us?" the she-wolf asks, her eyes wide with shock.

"Yes. I wasn't about to let my pack mate rape an innocent she-wolf." Caden answers, coming to sit beside me. His scent wraps around me once more, and I take a moment to breathe it in. I am still mad at him, but I can't hide the fact that I relish being covered in his scent.

"There is a tree house up ahead, you can hide in and signal for help if you'd like us to help you there." I suggest to the pair, watching as the male tenderly holds onto the she-wolf. I can see the love in their eyes, my heart longing for the same type of love they have

"We were actually heading there when that wolf showed up. We were separated at the beginning of The Run and finally found each other. Our goal was to consummate our mating and make it official." The male states, his gaze never leaving the female. I smile at the two, happy to know they have found one another finally and relieved that there is some good in this event for couples.

"I am Lisa, Lisa McNiel and future Alpha of Crater Paw. This is Daniel Nodel, a warrior from my pack." Lisa introduces herself. Daniel chuckles, placing a soft kiss on Lisa's cheek before he looks at my small group.

"I guess after today, I will be her Luna." He states with pride, causing me and Caden to chuckle as I look at Amelia, who is in a similar situation with Bryden.

"I am Grace, and the she-wolf is Amelia. We are from Silver Birch, and Amelia will be the next Alpha as well, and I will be her Beta." I introduce myself and Amelia to the two before pointing to Caden.

"And this is Caden, future Alpha of Wœlf Haven." I continue, watching Caden stiffen for a moment before sending me a smile of gratitude. Whatever secrets he is hiding, I will not reveal them to these wolves. I will be the first person to learn his secrets, or he can forget about our first date ever happening.

After making sure Lisa and Daniel can walk, we helped the two to the tree house and made sure they were safe. Caden once again shifts into his wolf form, letting me climb onto his back. With a nod, we are off once more, and I contemplate the kind of relationship I would want with Caden once I learn his secrets.

Chapter 34 Caden

———

My mind is racing as my paws carry me closer to the Lodge. It won't be long till Grace wins the bet and I can claim the title that is rightfully mine. I know she will demand answers from me as soon as we are safe, and I am terrified that Grace will come to resent me once she knows the truth. But she also deserves the truth if she is going to decide whether she is still willing to date me or not. I let out a sigh, still conscious of her clinging to me as I refuse to let her run while still injured and slow my pace. We have been running for hours now and will need to rest soon.

Suddenly, I feel the weight of Grace's body shift on top of me and come to a stop, afraid she will fall off and hurt herself further. Her even breathing settles what little panic has risen inside me, and I smile, letting out a huff of breath that resembles a chuckle. She has fallen asleep on top of me, and I couldn't be any happier. She still trusts me enough to let down her guard and fall asleep around me.

Amelia comes to a stop beside me, letting out a yawn as she stretches her body. I can tell that she, too, is tired, and to be honest, so am I. With the Lodge only being a few hours away, I decide that resting for a bit will be best. We do not know how many desperate wolves will be blocking the final path to freedom as they fight to claim a mate - and with Amelia and Grace both being un-mated, they will need their strength to fight these wolves head-on.

Pressing my head against Amelia's shoulder, I nod towards the left where I scented fresh water. I know there is a pond with a creek nearby, meaning a cave is most likely close by as well. She nods, understanding my meaning, and the two of us take off at a slow trot. Conscious of the now sleeping Grace on top of me, I am careful not to make any sudden movements in case she slips off. Moments later, we come face to face with the pond.

Amelia quickly rushes into the water and begins splashing around like a pup. I shake my head, wanting to laugh at her playfulness, before following the small creek, where thankfully I find a cave nearby.

Taking a deep breath near the entrance, I try to scent any wolves or fledgling Vampires that could be resting inside, and after scenting nothing out of the ordinary and feeling confident that the cave is safe for the night, I walk inside and take in the surroundings.

Inside is the usual mattress, and instead of a bag full of survival items, a small metal chest is placed to the side. Carefully, I maneuver Grace off my back and shift, taking the bag off her back slowly so as not to wake her before scooping her into my arms and helping her lie in a more comfortable position before covering her with the thin blanket left at the foot of the mattress.

Moving my attention to the bag, I quickly grab the pair of shorts and slide them on before walking out of the cave and scanning the pond for Amelia. I spot her quickly, the she-wolf lying by the edge of the water basking in the moonlight, and chuckle. She is carefree like a pup, and it really balances out Grace's serious attitude.

"Amelia!" I call out, watching her head pop up from her paws as she looks in my direction, puzzled. Waving my arm, I disappear into the cave once more, knowing she will be coming in shortly. I take this time to check the contents of the metal chest, the lid opening with ease and not making much sound. I hear the soft tap, tap, tap of nails on stone and turn my head towards the entrance just as Amelia walks in, her fur still damp from playing in the water.

Turning my focus back to the chest, I rummage inside to find some long, baggy shirts and canned food. Smiling triumphantly, I throw a shirt at Amelia, watching her catch the fabric between her teeth before she disappears outside. I shake my head again in amusement at the blonde she-wolf before returning my attention to the chest and taking out two cans of mixed fruit for the two of us to eat.

"Something other than jerky?" Amelia asks as she re-enters the cave, taking a spot on the mattress as I walk towards the blonde. Handing her a can of the fruit, I carefully sit beside Grace and watch the rise and fall of her chest as she sleeps.

"No, there is a bag of that inside the chest, but I thought we could use something different." I answer, cracking open the can of fruit and tipping the contents into my mouth. Amelia shrugs before digging into her can, a look of satisfaction on her face.

"Should we wake Grace up?" I ask, wanting to make sure she eats as well.

"No. She needs her sleep." Amelia answers with a sigh, looking at the sleeping wolf between us. I nod in agreement, finishing my food quickly and placing the can off to the side. I feel the exhaustion from running hours on end creeping in, and the thought of curling up beside Grace seems like a good idea.

Lying on the outer side of the mattress, I pull the sleeping wolf gently to my side and wrap my arms around Grace protectively as Amelia stretches out on the side of the mattress, resting against the cave wall and in an instant falls asleep. Holding in a chuckle, I bury my nose in Grace's hair and breathe in her scent as sleep takes hold of me.

Chapter 35 Grace

The scent of the forest in winter surrounds me once more, making my slowly waking body want nothing more than to fall back asleep wrapped in this scent. Strong arms that I know to be Caden's keep me snuggled tight against him, and although I am mad at him for keeping things from me, I don't fight to get free. The steady beating of his heart under my head reminds me that, other than to win the bet, I have something else to look forward to. Learning who Caden truly is and maybe a possible first date.

Opening my eyes, I turn my head to look up at Caden, his right arm covering his eyes as he sleeps peacefully. I can see the dark circles peeking out from under, knowing that all of us have been through so much in the seven days we have been here. Today will be our last day to make it to the Lodge, and from there, we can get all the rest we will need.

Carefully sliding out of Caden's hold, I climb off the mattress and stretch while checking to see if my body is good enough to run again. I want to finish this bet with my Alpha on my own without being carried over the magic barrier that encases the forest. Turning to look at my friends, I smile and decide to let them sleep a little longer and head outside the cave.

The sun is just starting to rise over the treetops, casting a warm orange glow over the pond. It is a beautiful sight compared to the deep blue hue the moon casts in the night, and I think about how today will be my last day here in the forest, my last day to ever participate in The Run. Within a few hours, I will be victorious in the bet, and Silver Birch's Alpha will be Amelia and I her Beta. I lean against the cave entrance, allowing the peaceful forest to wash over me as someone stirs within the cave. Soon, arms pull me close to their owner, and I find myself once more being held by Caden.

"Penny for your thoughts?" Asks Caden in a whisper, placing a gentle kiss on top of my head.

"I was just thinking about how this will be our last day." I answer quietly, getting a chuckle in response.

"It's been one hell of a week, Grace, but I am glad I got to spend it with Amelia and you." I smile at his words, hearing the gentleness in his voice as he takes a deep breath, inhaling my scent. We stand in the entrance, enjoying the calmness of the dawn, allowing us to just enjoy the moment. If The Run wasn't such a horrible event for she-wolves, this forest would make a lovely place for young wolves to meet with others and fall in love.

"Do you think The Run will ever end?" I ask, turning to look at Caden, only to find his emerald eyes already trained on me.

"I do. I have a feeling this will be the last one by the end of today." He answers, his eyes holding a flame of determination within them. Something deep inside me tells me that this is the truth and hope for a better future for all she-wolves lights inside me. After a moment of silence spanning between us, Caden leads me back into the cave, where we find Amelia awake and dividing up the leftover food from the bag Airia gave me. Taking a seat on the mattress, I thank Amelia as she passes me my portion of the food and promptly get to eating. We won't be stopping for any breaks as we race to the Lodge, and finishing any and all food that can give us the energy needed to fight off any attackers is a good idea.

"I will be running with the two of you." I state, catching Amelia and Caden off guard, as my friends look at me in shock.

"Are you sure? I don't mind you riding on my back." Caden asks, his left hand reaching out and taking my right.

"I am sure. My body has rested long enough, and I need to finish this bet with my Alpha on my own terms." I answer, leaving no room for arguments. Caden lets out a sigh, a brief moment of disappointment flashing in his eyes. Thankfully, they don't fight my decision, and after our breakfast, we all shift to our wolves. I look at the bag Princess Airia gave me, wondering if I should take it with me or not, when Caden picks it up between his teeth. With a yip of excitement from Amelia, the three of us leave the cave and rush towards the direction of the Lodge. I have a bet to win, and I'll be damned if I let the tension between Caden and me ruin it.

Chapter 36 Caden

⸻

I growl as a wolf comes too close to Grace on my right, the dirty brown wolf facing the blunt of the power coursing through my blood. He whimpers, instantly lowering himself to the ground in submission, indicating he understands that I can rip him to shreds in an instant if he continues to grow closer to the silver wolf. We have been running for two hours now since leaving the cave, and in those two hours, we have crossed paths with numerous wolves, either rushing to claim a mate or rushing to the Lodge for their freedom.

I watch as Grace dodges another wolf – a grey wolf – trying to sweep her paws out from under her. Smile as I watch as she whips around and bites on his jugular and growls menacingly at him. He submits to her, showing his neck and slowly lowering his body to the ground. She knows not to rip his throat open, but her display of power shows the male that she can and will destroy him if he tries anything.

Satisfied with the grey wolf's submission, Grace lets him go before running and returning to my side. Pride swells inside me at the strength Grace has, knowing that I have found my perfect match.

We nod to one another, a mutual understanding that as we race through the last of the forest, we will need to rely on one another to make it safely across the veil of magic that surrounds the Moon Goddess's forest. A she-wolf emerges from Amelia's right, her grey wolf frantically rushing towards us. I can see relief in her eyes as if asking if we will help her to safety.

Unfortunately, as she is about to join our trio, a male rushes out from behind, tackling the she-wolf to the ground. Amelia's steps falter, a look of panic in her eyes. I can tell she wants to help the she-wolf, but it is too late. The male has already positioned himself inside the she-wolf, the smell of lust and sex floating off of the two. He has claimed his mate, and interfering now would result in Grace or Amelia being captured by someone else.

With a look of regret, Amelia pushes forward and flanks my right side. I give her a small nod, knowing that the decision not to help that she-wolf was a hard one to make, but I am happy she decided her safety comes first.

A yelp of pain to my right has me skidding to a stop and turning to see Amelia being tackled by a black wolf, his massive body covering her blonde one as he lunges for the scruff of her neck. Before I can react, a blur of silver has already slammed her body into the black wolf, and I watch as Grace lunges for the man's throat, sinking her teeth into it and drawing blood. Her anger radiates off of her as I rush to help Amelia up, checking for any mate mark and happy to find that other than ruffled fur, she is fine.

The black wolf submits to Grace, her furious growls rumbling over us until she finally releases the male, baring her teeth at him in warning. She pads over to Amelia, checking her friend over before giving me a quick lick on the cheek, most likely in thanks for helping Amelia while she took care of the male. With a nudge to her friend, Grace takes off again, Amelia behind her and me taking the rear.

I want to release the power within me to scare all these males away from my friends, but then that would cause a chain reaction of events that I am not ready to deal with yet. Instead, I heighten my senses and keep a lookout for any males trying to sneak in and take Grace or Amelia as their own, growling and snapping my fangs at anyone who gets too close. The wind blows towards us, bringing the scent of hundreds of wolves and the shimmering of the veil can be seen ahead. We were close.

Close to the goal of Grace winning the bet.

Close to Amelia becoming the Alpha of her pack after we cross the veil.

Close to me claiming what is rightfully mine.

Chapter 37 Grace

⸻

Vultures.

That's how I would describe these desperate males as they see a lone she-wolf rushing to cross the veil of the Run. Like vultures scenting a carcass in the desert, the moment the males scent a female, they descend on her and fight to mate with her. As soon as a male inserts himself inside her, the others back away, knowing that the she-wolf has been claimed and slink off to find another victim. I feel pity for the poor girls, every fibre of my being wanting to run back and save them, but that would lead me to being claimed if I am not careful.

The sun had begun to set a few minutes ago, the sky a vibrant mix of red, orange and yellow. I have until midnight to cross the veil when the magic in the moon recedes for the next six months until The Run returns. I can see the wolves waiting on the other side, some unmated wanting to see the action, some mated waiting to see if their friends can score a mate.

My paws thunder against the earth as I push myself forward, moving faster and faster with my race against time and the desperate need to win the bet that will help my pack mates. Victory is within reach, and soon I will be taking my father's precious Beta position away from him, and there is nothing he can do about it.

[Grace, we are so close!] Amelia calls out through our link, yapping happily. I can see the veil of magic shimmering, the Moon Goddess letting this be her way of showing us out of the cage they call The Run. I howl excitedly, my companions doing the same as we announce our victory in completing The Run without being claimed or claiming another.

[My father is there, I can see the look of shock on his face and the rage on your father beside him.] Amelia calls out with laughter in her words. Inwardly, I smirk, zeroing in on my father, who is seething with rage. He must see Caden's golden wolf between Amelia and me and know that we have been travelling with a strong male – a male that could have claimed either of us but didn't.

Cheers from my pack thundered in the air behind our Alpha, ignoring my father as he shouts at them when they chant my name. Word of the bet must have travelled around, as every last one of my pack mates who despise this event lined up ready to accept my triumph. As soon as I cross the border, no one in Silver Birch will be forced into The Run ever again. I am only a few meters from the border now.

My attention shifts to the right as twigs snap loudly, the sense of danger towards Amelia, my Alpha and sister, coming from that direction. Without thinking, I rush towards Amelia, leaping just in time to intercept a grey wolf that was just about to tackle my friend. Our bodies tangle in a flurry of claws and fangs and fur, being ripped by one another. Caden turns around, his intention clear when he rushes towards me, but I snarl at him, my head motioning to Amelia, who is just rushing towards him. The grey wolf takes my distraction as an opportunity to throw me off of his body, a yelp of pain escaping me when my shoulder hits the ground hard before he rushes off towards Amelia.

Caden changes course, his golden body grabbing onto Amelia's scruff before he takes off towards the border. The grey wolf is still in pursuit, and I force myself to stand, to run and tackle the grey wolf once more. We go tumbling to the ground with our claws scraping against each other's flanks, the scent of blood filling my nose. The only thought running through my mind right now is screw the bet, I have to protect my Alpha.

Gasps from the spectators watch as the male and I struggle to dominate the other. My grip on his neck never loosens while he does everything he can to be rid of me. Without warning, his teeth manage to sink into my paw, the feeling of my bones snapping under his bite and blood gushing from the wound forces me to release my jaw from the scruff of his neck and fall to the ground.

I whimper, standing to my feet and snarl at this male. He is an Alpha, his blood radiating the power of one who will soon be inheriting a pack. Every instinct in me wants me to submit to him, to allow this Alpha to win, but I harden myself and prepare for the next round of our fight.

Finally, he moves and I wait as he jumps into the air, his intention of tackling me clear as day, before I run, sliding under his airborne body and turning around quickly enough to claw his side and soft underbelly, giving him a severe wound. Hearing the high-pitched yelp as this wolf falls to the ground, I take this opportunity to rush over to his injured body and sink my teeth into the tender spot of his neck deep enough to cause harm but not deep enough to kill him. He shifts, intending to throw me off again, but he does not understand the precarious position he is in.

Sinking my teeth further into his skin and using my injured paw to claw at the open wound on his underbelly, I growl in warning, threatening more damage to this wolf if he does not submit. After a brief moment of pause, the grey wolf sticks his neck out as best as he can in submission, letting me know I have won.

I pull away with another growl, letting him know that I will end him if he tries any underhanded tricks before turning and limping my way towards the veil.

"Grace, you can do it!" Amelia shouts encouragingly, her body wrapped in Bryden's embrace as the two cheer me on. I send a wolfish grin her way, my vision becoming blurry with the pain from the battle and blood loss. I feel my body sway for a moment before I stumble, doing my best to keep going until I feel my legs give out.

Lying on the ground, a shadow covers my body, and I growl. But the truth is, I am too injured to fight; my body covered in claw marks, leaking blood. This male before me will claim me easily, and there is nothing I can do to stop him.

With a sigh, I close my eyes, waiting to be claimed until a long tongue brushes the spot between my eyes. Shocked, I open my sapphire orbs to see Caden licking at my injured paw, worry in his emerald eyes. Relief that it is him coming to my side fills me, and I do not fight him when he picks me up by the scruff, his teeth gentle yet his hold firm.

Curling my body into a ball, I allow him to carry me and do my best not to get in the way of his paws. The magic of the veil passes over our body, and the little strength I have seeps away. The Run is over for me and Caden. I have won the bet and made it out of this Goddess-forsaken forest without being claimed and mated. With that thought in mind, I closed my eyes and let darkness take me as I drifted off to sleep.

Chapter 38 Caden

Ignoring the wolves stepping forward with their intentions of helping Grace, I growl at their outstretched hands until they back away in fear. By their scent, I know they are her packmates, but my instinct to protect the woman I want as my mate is strong. My blood is boiling, the scene of her falling to the ground bleeding after defeating that male replaying in my mind.

I want to tear into him, kill him for touching my Lady Silver and wounding her, but I stopped myself as getting her across the veil and to the medical ward was more important. Wolves feeling the power in my blood skitter away and give me a clear path to the medical wing, a building just newly built a few years ago after the many wolves being found injured within the forest after The Run. The door is wide open as I storm in, my tail flicking with worry for the limp she-wolf in my grasp.

"Master Caden, so nice-"

[Just heal her.] I mind-linked the doctor, taking down all of the barriers from my mind and cutting him off as my power radiated off of me in waves. It is time for me to be who I truly am. It is time for me to show Grace who I am meant to be and show her the future she will have with me if she allows it. The doctor and his staff get to work, carefully taking Grace's body and lifting the silver wolf onto a gurney before whisking her away to the nearest surgical room.

"Caden!" Someone shouts for me in anger, and I frown. I know that voice all too well, and judging by the tone, my father is not happy with me. With a growl of annoyance, I whirl around to face the man that I plan to kill, and soon.

"You insufferable fool!" Gregory growls out as soon as he nears me.

"You had two she-wolves to choose from, and neither holds your scent!" I growl at his words, not liking the tone he is giving me. Glaring at the man I sadly have to share the same DNA with and call my father, I cannot wait for the moment my teeth sink into his jugular and life fades from his eyes. My father – the Alpha of the Royal Pack and King of Werewolves – is on borrowed time now.

"Don't you growl at me, you filth. This was your last chance to bring home a mate and proper Alpha Queen. Now I'll make Felix my heir." He leers at me, taking a step back. My blood is boiling from the rage he is fueling, the power of a Royal Wolf surging towards him. I know he has grown weaker over the years, his reign loosening as the wolves he commands shift their allegiance to me. Soon, the title of King will be mine, but not yet. Right now, I need to focus on Grace and make sure she is taken care of. Allowing the shift to take over, I feel my golden fur recede into my skin as my body rearranges itself before I stand in front of my father in my human form.

"You're not worth arguing with right now." I calmly state, letting the anger and power radiate in my words and relish in the shiver of fear the man who gave me life tries to conceal from me.

"Grace needs me, and by her side is where I'll be. When I know she's going to make a full recovery, be prepared to lose your title, Alpha King." My eyes glow gold in the sign of a challenge, the fear in my father's eyes growing. He knows I am serious, that I am ready to kill him and rid the evil stain he has left on werewolf kind. With a growl of warning, I turn on my heels and follow Grace's scent.

The scent leads me to the back, where the double doors reading surgical room greet me. As I reach out to open the door, it suddenly opens, and a nurse walks out, her black hair pulled back into a bun.

"Caden." She calls out, shocked. I smile at Karina Randall as I peer over her shoulder to see if I can catch a glimpse inside the room.

"Hey Riri, I am not in the mood right now, so if you will step aside." I greet my half sister half heartedly. A nurse moves to the side as he fixes the blanket, and I finally get a glimpse of Grace. Her silver hair is brushed out across her pillow, and I wonder when she had shifted back to her human form.

"I see someone has a case of puppy love." Karina coos at me jokingly, mischief in her eyes. I growl warningly at her, not in the mood to deal with my little sister's teasing while I try to push past her into the room. She steps in front of me, giving me a pointed look as I glare at her for getting in my way, letting another growl slip past my lips.

"That is a sterile room, Caden. We can't risk you interrupting the doctor, so go take a shower and change into some clean clothes." Gone is my playful sister as she uses her own Alpha tone against me, her power, although muted because of her mother's blood, washing over my body like a feather tickling me. I am annoyed at her for getting between me and the woman I have fallen for, but she is right. Right now, Grace is being tended to, and if I were to barge in now, it could impede her treatment.

With an annoyed growl, I take one final look at Grace's sleeping face before barging towards the men's locker room. I walk past the lockers and to the back where the showers wait, quickly turning on the water and focusing on scrubbing my body clean.

My mind wanders back to Grace tackling that grey wolf. How she fought to protect Amelia and help the she-wolf she calls her sister and Alpha cross the veil. How she snarled at me for wanting to help her before I ultimately helped Amelia in her stead.

I did not hesitate to throw Amelia across the veil, knowing that once I crossed, I would not be able to enter the forest again. I watched as a man caught Amelia midair, the blond shifting as she kissed him happily before pulling away from him and reminding me to save Grace. I didn't need any reminding, as once I knew Amelia was safe, I rushed back to Grace just in time to watch the male submit to her and her falling down. She is a fighter, my Grace, and I can't help but both admire and fear her fierce nature. She could have been claimed had I not managed to make it to her side and carry her across the veil.

Slamming my fist against the tiled wall and cracking it into shards, I finish my shower and step out of the stall. Grabbing the nearest towel, I quickly dry myself while exiting the shower area and into the locker room.

To the right of me is a shelf, full of clean clothes sorted by size. I quickly grab a clean set of clothes from the pile on the shelves to throw on. As I am just about to leave the room, I walk past the mirrors and notice my shoulder-length hair and the messy facial hair that has grown. I know I shouldn't care about my appearance, but after making sure Grace is fine, I will be taking on my father and claiming the title Alpha King, and I need to look the part of a Royal if I am to succeed in capturing the loyalty of the crowd.

With a sigh, I search the shelves and find some disposable razors, taking the time to shave my face before tying back the top half of my hair. I won't be able to cut it until I return home, so this will have to do for now.

After a final look in the mirror, I throw away the razor and walk into the hallway. The surgical room is empty, and after finding a nurse to inquire about Grace, who I learn is on the mend and doing better, I make my way to her room.

The medical ward is filled with nurses and doctors rushing about helping those in need who have left the forest, and I do my best to stay out of the way while walking closer to Grace's room, watching wolves being brought in by pack mates and coordinators.

Finally, I smell that sweet scent of hers and feel my heart beat. Hopefully, she is awake now, and I can explain everything to her. With a small smile, I turn the handle and push open the door, instantly getting hit with aggression in the air as a loud slap sounds against the four walls.

"You're a filthy bitch!"

Chapter 39 Grace

———

My cheek stings from the harsh slap my father gave me, his fury clear as day in the way his eyes stare at me. I glare back at him, wanting nothing more than to kill the bastard in front of me and end his sorry excuse for a life.

"You're a filthy bitch!" He screams out, spittle flying from his lips as he seethes in anger. I scoff, pressing a hand against my throbbing cheek to help calm the pain. This isn't the first time he has called me something derogatory.

"No, I'm not." I state, smirking as I look into his eyes.

"I won The Run and the bet without being mated." I continue with a chuckle, watching the fury in his eyes grow. I can tell I have pushed him to the edge as he clenches and unclenches his hands.

"No, you're a slut that kept Amelia away from that wolf." He counters, his nostril flaring. If looks could kill, I would be dead twice over by now.

"She could have been mated by now, and instead she is in the arms of that warrior because you butted into a situation that did not concern you!" He continues, his accusation screamed at me, and I just roll my eyes. I had seen Bryden holding onto Amelia when she called out to me before I collapsed, seen the worry in his eyes for me as he kept my chosen sister close and guarded from our fathers.

"At least she will have a proper mate to rule over Silver Birch with." I shrug, my nonchalant answer seeming to be the proverbial straw that breaks the camel's back as my father backs away, becoming unusually calm. My senses go on alert as I realize the danger he presents, and I wonder just what trick he will play.

"Maybe I should claim you instead." My father muses with a dark chuckle. I shudder, realizing that he is dead serious as he takes a step closer to my bed, his hands already reaching down to unbuckle the belt around his waist. I curse the pain medicine coursing through my blood, realizing how vulnerable they make me in this moment. Throwing the blanket off me, I get ready to run when a blur appears before me and my father is sent crashing into the wall behind him.

"Don't you dare think about touching her!" A violent growl leaves my saviour, and I recognize the person standing protectively before me as Caden. My beating heart settles, and I relax back into the bed as the fear that was growing instantly vanishes. With Caden around, I am safe.

"Who the hell do you think you are? That is my daughter, and as such, I can do anything I want to her." My father yells back, stepping up to Caden, ready to fight him.

"My name is Caden Silas Wolfrain Alcazaris. I am the Crown Prince and future Alpha King of all Werewolves." Caden states, the power of a Royal wolf seeping out of his body. My father's eyes widen, his anger at being disturbed turning into fear, and he cowers before Caden. He has made a grave mistake and knows that backing down and showing Caden his neck submissively, like he is doing now, is the right move. It is a sight I never thought I would ever see, but I can't help the satisfaction in watching my father cower before someone who is both younger and stronger.

Caden promised to tell me the truth yesterday, even though I had put everything together. The secrecy in how he acted, the not wanting to tell me anything until we arrived at the Lodge, all made sense now. How his father wanted him to claim a mate and why he helped other she-wolves. This was my Prince, the one who advocated for she-wolf rights.

"You have five seconds to disappear from our sight or I will execute you." Caden growls out, interrupting me from my thoughts. My father takes no time in rushing out as if a demon is chasing him, and I chuckle. It felt nice seeing him be so meek and not in control for once.

Silence settles in the room, and I wait patiently for Caden to calm down. The power coursing through his blood slowly settles until he turns to face me, the rage in his body now gone as he takes in my body lying on the hospital bed.

"Hey." He whispers shyly, rubbing the back of his neck. I laugh, seeing his small blush on his face as he carefully walks to my side and takes my hand. Gone is the Alpha Prince commanding the fear of the Goddess into a wolf. Now, he is the Caden I have grown to love, who spent days with me in the Run.

"What's so funny?" He questions with a pout, melting my heart as he brings my hand to his lips and places a gentle kiss on my knuckles.

"The big bad Alpha Prince becomes shy and meek in front of me." I state with a giggle, deciding that whatever explanation he is going to give me, I will accept with an open mind. I want this wolf, want him to love me and to love him back.

"I see." He chuckles out, letting go of my hand and sliding into bed with me. He pulls me close to his side; one arm wrapped around me while the other takes my right hand in his left. I smile, enjoying his scent wrapping itself into every inch of my skin as I lean into his body, resting my head against his chest.

"I'm sorry I kept my identity a secret from you." He sighs out placing a kiss on top of my head. I wrap my arm over his stomach, settling in closer to him and wait for Caden to continue.

"I spent my teen years having she-wolves throw themselves at me because they learned I am the Crown Prince. I got tired of trying to date, only to learn they are after me for my power and title. When I became eligible to enter The Run, I decided to keep my identity a secret from everyone and use my mother's pack as a cover." He continues, his hand fiddling with my hair. I let his words sink in, and in the end, I know that although hiding his true identity hurt me, it was a necessary action for him to find a she-wolf that would be true to Caden for who he is. With a smile, I lift my head and place a soft kiss on his chin.

"I understand, Caden. I wish you had told me from the start because power and titles do not mean anything to me." I can see the tension leaving his body from my words as his eyes stay locked onto mine.

"I was upset when I realized you were hiding something from me, but knowing you only did so in order not to be taken advantage of makes sense. I am not mad anymore." Without warning, Caden pulls me in for a kiss, his soft lips pouring so much emotion into mine. My eyes close on their own as I kiss him back, the kiss deepening as soon as I do. It ends all too soon, and I am left trying to catch my breath when Caden and I pull apart. The tension between us is gone now. Snuggling into his side once more, I enjoy the peaceful silence as his fingers play with my hair.

"I have something I need to tell you too." I state, blushing, opening my eyes to see him staring at me.

"I already figured out you have powers, Grace. It's not like you tried to hide them from my view." He chuckles, making me smile. He is right, though. During our time in the forest, I used my powers to sense the Ragers and any other threat.

"You can tell me all about them when you are ready, Lady Silver, so don't worry." He adds, pressing a soft kiss on my forehead.

"Okay, sounds good Caden." I agree softly, content for once in my life.

"Do you still want to go on that date?" He asks, his fingers pausing.

"Yes. But you have to plan it." I answer, letting out a yawn. Caden chuckles, placing another soft kiss on my forehead before he tightens his arms around me.

"Deal. And I promise never to hide anything from you ever again." With a soft sigh, I close my eyes and decide that as long as I have Caden beside me, I can go through anything life throws at me.

Chapter 40 Caden

The early morning sun filters into the room, waking me from my sleep. I smile as I take a deep breath, the air being filled with the scent of lavender and mint. Curled into my side, Grace sleeps soundly in my arms, and I can't help but stare at her serene face, her eyelids fluttering as she dreams.

Today is the day after The Run came to an end. There will be meetings between the Alphas and coordinators as many plan to initiate their new pack mates into their packs. The best part of today is that Grace, Amelia and I have survived The Run. Now I have a date to plan for the woman wrapped in my embrace.

I smile, thinking about how I plan to romance the she-wolf in my arms, to show her a side of me that I have dreamed of giving a woman. She sees me as Caden, the friend she made in The Run and not as Alpha Prince Caden, the man who will rule all the wolves in the world. I never thought that the day someone who loves me for me would come, but here it is.

Making sure that Grace is sound asleep, I slowly untangle her from my body and slide off the bed. As much as I would love to stay curled up beside her, I have something that needs to be done.

[Zander, is everyone ready?] I ask, linking my Beta.

[Yes, Alpha, we are all in place, ready to commence the operation.] I smirk, pausing at the door to look back at Grace. I made her a promise that The Run will end, and after this morning, I will be putting effort into creating a better future for wolf kind. With a deep breath and inhaling in Grace's calming scent that I have grown to love once more, I step out of the room and close the door.

"Zander told me to stand guard over the she-wolf inside." Karina greets me, her nurse uniform gone and replaced with a slick black outfit. I nod, thank my sister for protecting Grace in my stead, and silently make my way out of the medical ward.

Wolves are gathering outside, some making their way to the front of the Lodge, and I follow. A stage has been erected since last night, and on velvet chairs sat my father, Felix, and the Ancient Vampire Eli. It seems I am just in time for the celebrations to start.

"Greeting participants of the Run and visiting Alphas." A voice calls out, the announcer from seven days ago standing proud at the podium.

"The Run has concluded this cycle, and many events have occurred. First, congratulations to those who have gained a mate." Cheers from those now mated rang through the crowd, and I suppress a snarl. How can wolves cheer when many she-wolves were beaten and rapped. She-wolves that will be whisked to a new pack and taken away from their loved ones.

"Okay, settle down now." The announcer chuckles, amusement flickering over his face as he scans the crowd. He waits, the cheers slowly dying down before taking a deep breath.

"Next, Ancient Eli has confirmed that all of the rogue fledglings have been killed. We are happy that no one was killed by them, and thank those who helped in eliminating those fledgling, you are all brave men and women. He has already seen the recordings of the kills and has prepared awards for those who have killed a Fledgling." Another round of cheering erupts from the crowd, and I think of Grace lying in bed, sleeping peacefully. She had killed one on her own and definitely deserves praise. Zander, Cody, Caleb, Mike and Amelia deserve their rewards as well. The five of them put up a good fight. The announcer settles everyone once more, a look of pride on his face as he calls attention to him once more.

"Finally, as you all may have noticed, we have another guest with us. Please welcome our Alpha King, King Gregory Alcazaris, as he has an important announcement to make." It is time. I watch as my father stands, his face set in a friendly mask, but I know the true evil that hides behind his perfectly practiced smiles. The mounds of bodies from dead she-wolves that have gotten too close to him and try to claim their spot as Alpha Queen by trying to use their pregnancies against him. The multitude of rogues he captured and hunted as sport.

The crowd bows to him in respect, and I scoff, wanting nothing more than to rush up there and kill the man who gave me life.

"You may all rise." His deep voice echoes over the crowd as if he were some magnanimous person and not a monster that will execute a wolf just for bringing him lukewarm coffee.

"Many of you are wondering why I am here, and as you all know, I have yet to appoint my heir and the next Alpha King." He starts, his smile fading into a frown. I watch as Felix lets out a smug smile, and dread fills me. That bastard plans to give the throne to Felix and announce it here and now.

[Now?] Caleb asks, his anger towards my father evident in his voice.

[No. Let him dig his own grave.] I answer, feeling Zander walking up behind me, ready to protect me if need be.

"As such, I have decided with a heavy heart that my son will not be appointed as heir, but instead I have chosen someone else. I am highly disappointed that for the last six years, my son Prince Caden Alcazaris has had twelve opportunities to bring home a mate. Instead, he decided to prevent our males from bringing home perfectly good she-wolves and ruined any mating-"

"Mating?!" I shout out, cutting my father's speech off, already done with his bullshit.

"If by mating you mean kidnapping, raping, and murder, then you are right, I refuse to be a part of this!" I shout back, seeing wolves nod in agreement. Taking slow, measured steps, I keep my senses on high alert as I watch my father fume with anger at my interruption.

"Caden, stand down!" My father growls with rage, the power of his blood turning his words into a command. Glaring back at him, I scoff, his command weak and brushing past me like a soft breeze. I no longer saw him as my Alpha the moment I decided I would challenge him for the throne, meaning his command barely affects me like it used to.

"I will not stand down!" I shout back, letting my own blood boil with the power of a Royal Alpha wolf. I watch my father flinch, seeing the realization that I am stronger than him hitting him hard. It seems I will be able to succeed in killing this bastard.

"The Run may have passed a hundred years ago when women were considered property and could be claimed easily, but that isn't the case now." I continue, seeing some wolves agree while others scoff at me, calling me a wimp of a man. I ignore those wolves and instead I focus on the ones agreeing with me, with many being she-wolves.

"He's right!" Someone shouts from the crowd, and I hold back my smirk as I recognize the voice as Amelia. Befriending her and keeping her safe was my luckiest moment in The Run.

"We live in a world where women now have rights. Where they can own their own homes and businesses and do whatever they want. Why should we allow them to run for their lives and allow a man to rape them?" A male's voice calls out in the same direction as Amelia, one I believe belongs to Bryden, Amelia's boyfriend. The crowd begins to voice their agreement, some woman shouting they don't want their mate, others claiming they were unjustly raped. I watch as my father tries to calm the crowd, his eyes widening as he realizes I am winning the people he rules over.

"I think it's time we enter into a new era, one where she-wolves have equal rights as males and can choose their mates based on love. It's time we stop forcing our people to run in a forest with fear of being rape or fear of losing their rightful title if they do not rape and bring a she-wolf back as their mate!" I shout, allowing the wolves to shout their agreement for change. To a world with equal opportunity for she-wolves. Zander squeezes my shoulder, his silent support reminding me that he has my back as my Beta, and I send a thank you through our link.

"It's time for a change, and it starts with a change in rulers." The wolves that gather around me cheer, and I smile. I will take the crown from my father and rule, whether or not I have a mate beside me.

"Caden, I am warning you. Felix is my chosen heir, and I will not take your insolence!" Gregory roars out, silencing the crowd. Felix smirks from his seat, not bothering to stand beside my father, and I laugh. How can anyone be loyal to a wolf who refuses to stand beside the man who made him the next heir?

"Felix will never be the heir because I, Caden Silas Wolfrain Alcazaris, challenge you, King Gregory Otto Alcazaris, to the title of Alpha King!" My eyes meet my father's with a steady hatred, knowing the emerald green of my iris has turned gold once more in a challenge. I wait, wondering if Gregory will take the challenge. With a roar, he rushes off the stage, shifting mid-air into his black and grey wolf.

Pushing Zander back, I roll to the left and shift into my golden wolf, thankfully dodging Gregory's attack. The crowd backs up, creating a wide circle around the two of us and giving us room to fight. I snarl as Gregory stands, shaking out his fur while his emerald eyes – the only thing inherited from him - stare back at me with fury.

We circle each other, trying to find a weakness in one another that we can exploit to gain the upper hand. As if a bell has rung, we spring towards one another in a clash of claws and teeth, trying to find some hold. I feel the claws of his right paw graze my shoulder and take note that he is favouring his left side. A weakness he was trying to hide from me. Swiping my claws against his face, I back away and allow him to regain his bearings as blood drips down the right side of his muzzle.

As he shakes his head, most likely to regain his focus from the pain, I study his left side, trying to find his weak spot. Gregory charges at me, his right eye closed, and I quickly side step to the left, using my momentum to sink my teeth into his right shoulder. He howls with pain, the crunch of bone letting me know I have broken his shoulder cap. He whips his body to the side, forcing me to let go and duck just in time to dodge a swipe at my head.

With him balancing on his hind legs, I push off from the ground and tackle Gregory to the ground and sink my canines into his neck. He struggles, his hind legs kicking at my underbelly and leaving wounds, but I ignore the pain as I force myself to shred his jugular with my canines. He whimpers, his kicks slowly growing weaker as the blood in his body drains from the wound I am slowly making bigger.

[Are you really going to kill me?] His voice fills my mind, and by the silence of the crowd, they have heard him as well.

[Yes, because if I don't, you will find a way to keep The Run going and ruin any chance at a better future for all of us.] I answer, my voice cold and emotionless. I stopped considering this man my father years ago, stopped caring about him and only focused on my training to become King. I will not allow Gregory to ruin our nation by handing the care of all the wolves to Felix. I will not allow our people to be raped and enslaved by males because of a long-standing tradition.

Gregory growls, his weak kicks landing a blow to my underbelly, causing me to wince and nearly lose my grip on his throat. Furious, I paw at the broken shoulder and smirk at his pain-filled howls. Death is near for him, and I debate on whether or not I should make it quick and painless or long and painful. So many wolves died at his hands, some because they made a small mistake, some for being born. I think of the many half-siblings that never even lived past their first breaths because of his inability to keep his dick in his pants.

[Kill him already!] Karina's voice fills my mind, and I pause, thinking of the only sibling I have alive. She grew up in fear of this man, fear that one day he would snap and kill her or worse, mate her. I protected my sister, sending her away during the summers to my mother's pack, keeping Gregory away from her when he was angry and taking the beatings that were meant for her, knowing he would have killed my sister if given the chance. Karina is right, I need to end him.

Releasing my grip on his neck, I shift back into my skin and allow my nails to become claws. I can see the fear in Gregory's eyes, and ignore the pleading to let him live echoing in my mind through the link. I send a silent prayer to the Moon Goddess, asking her to let him suffer in the afterlife before plunging my clawed hand into his chest.

Gregory tries to kick out but fails, the blood loss making him too weak to fight back, while my hand reaches past his rib cage until I grasp the beating heart of his. Leaning forward, I look into his eyes, relishing in the fear and realization on his face that his only son is the one to end his life. With a smirk, I slowly crush his heart.

"Long live the King." I whisper loud enough for only Gregory to hear before I yank out his beating heart, ending his life. The crowd is silent, the shock of their tyrant of a ruler, whose beliefs are still set in the old ways, being defeated must be incredible. I close my eyes, allowing myself to mourn my father for the briefest moment before raising my hand, still clutching his heart in the air, the blood dripping down my forearm, and the cheers of the crowd roar into the air. I smile, taking in my victory and planning for the future. The wind blows the scent of mint and lavender towards me, and my smile grows, turning around knowing Grace just watched me defeat my father and her Alpha King.

"Caden behind you!" She shouts just as my body is tackled to the ground.

Chapter 41 Grace

A scrawny, tawny wolf tackles Caden, his jaws snapping at the man I love, but Caden manages to dodge it and even manages to hold back this scrawny wolf's face from taking a bite of him with his bare hands. Furious, I find myself moving, my steps turning into a run, and before I know it, I have shifted into my silver wolf and am tackling the intruder away from my Caden. The wolf rolls harshly onto the ground while I stand protectively between him and Caden, my fury boiling at the coward who tackled the newly named Alpha King from behind. Something tells me this is Felix, the cousin Caden mentioned a few days ago.

The tawny wolf regains his footing, shakes out the dirt and dust from his fur, before turning to growl at me. He is frustrated that I interfered, but so what? He is the one who attacked Caden without a challenge. I watch his every move, waiting to see when he will attack, and I don't have to wait too long. With clear intentions of where he is going to strike, I dodge to my right as he lunges for my throat, using my momentum and whirling around to land a blow to his flank with my claw. Felix stumbles, leaving an opening for me to lunge this time, and my teeth sink into his throat just enough to wound this coward.

By law, as the wolf to defend the wolf who was blind sided by an attacker, I have every right to kill Felix as his cowardly actions have brought shame to his pack. But I want to give Caden a chance to decide his cousin's fate. Felix snarls, flailing around trying to dislodge me, acting like an impudent pup, the embarrassment of being overpowered by a she-wolf being too much for him to bear. Rolling my eyes, I sweep out both his front paws from under him and follow as the front of his body falls to the ground, keeping my grip on his throat and letting a low warning growl out. I have easily pinned this wolf; his paws being swatted away with my own as he tries a futile attempt to claw at me. Sooner or later, he will come to submit or be killed.

"Felix, it's over. Grace has won." Caden's voice is loud and clear, and Felix lets out a defeated sigh. He submits under me, doing his best to thrust his neck out in defeat. I wait, trying to see if there will be any trickery on his end before backing away. Feeling a gentle hand on my head and a soft touch combing through my fur, I smile wolfishly and lean into Caden's touch, happy to know he is safe.

"Shift Felix." Caden orders, the power of the Alpha King already infused into his words. It is a command no wolf could refuse, and I am just glad the command is directed at Felix. Looking at Felix in amusement as he tries to resist the command, I sit down and wag my tail. This wolf really is pathetic. Unfortunately for Felix, his bones begin snapping in and out of place, much to his fight against Caden's command, until finally a greasy-looking man with a scowl on his face sits before me, his scrawny body being nothing compared to the one Caden possesses.

"Go to hell, Caden. Your dad had already named me heir!" He spits out, causing a growl from me to come forth for disrespecting not only the new King but also the man I want to be with. I relish in satisfaction as fear flickers in Felix's eyes and stop my growling when he stays silent.

"Good, be very afraid of me, little man." I think, Caden chuckling at my reaction.

"And I challenged him fairly and won. I did the honourable thing by giving a public challenge, unlike you, who attacked me like the coward you are." Caden counters with a low growl. I feel the anger radiate off of him in waves, feel his blood boil with the new power, and carefully nuzzle his hand, trying to help him keep calm in front of so many wolves. We do not need an angry Royal losing control in front of innocent wolves.

"I should have been the Alpha King, not you! You're a pathetic man who can't even claim a mate!" Felix snaps back, making me glare and snarl at the weasel-like man once more for his continual disrespect towards Caden.

"Tell that whore to calm down. A woman should know her place." Felix snaps as he points a finger at me, one I gladly bite off and enjoy the sound of flesh tearing and bones snapping filling the air along with his screams of agonizing pain. Just as quickly as I bit it off, I throw the finger down in front of me and shred it, a smirk on my wolfish face as I enjoy watching Felix look at me with pure terror.

"Grace knows her place as a powerful Alpha and Beta blooded she-wolf and is a great warrior as well as the woman I intend to date." Caden calmly states, chuckling at my display of power, before he scratches behind my left ear.

"You, on the other hand, cousin, are a weak Alpha blooded wolf. A coward. And you know the punishment for attacking a wolf without a direct challenge." He continues, bending down and placing a kiss on top of my head. If a blush was able to appear under my fur, my face would be beet-red for everyone to see.

"Grace, if you would like, you may kill him." Caden finishes, a smirk on his lips as he backs away, letting me enjoy my prey. I turn to look back at him, my tail wagging happily, before I turn to look at Felix, the weasel of a man staring back with such open terror that I wonder if he might die of fright. I take one step towards him and am shocked as he clambers to his feet and takes off, his speed in human form surprising me. The crowd parts, not wanting to touch him, knowing he is mine to deal with.

"Are you going to go after him?" Caden asks, amused, and I roll my eyes as I softly pad after Felix, a trail of blood leaking from his finger leading me to the coward as he attempts to climb a tree. I watch in amusement, wondering if this idiot will realize he has company and watch as he falls on his ass for the tenth time.

Deciding he has stewed in his fear long enough, I growl and watch as his body straightens in fear. I can see his slight tremors, taste the anxiety and despair in the air and relish in knowing I will be ridding Caden of this trash of a person from his life. Stalking towards my prey, I raise my paw just as Felix turns around and slice open his neck. Blood spills out like a geyser, and I jump back, not wanting to get any of his filth on my fur.

I decide to let Felix have a slow, painful death, watching him from a few feet away to make sure he dies. He struggles, his hands clutching his neck to slow the bleeding, but the wound is fatal. Even if his werewolf healing were to kick in, it's too late.

Finally, his body falls against the tree he had been trying to climb, and his limbs go limp. I heighten my senses and let out a silent prayer that Felix may be reincarnated as a she-wolf and can experience the pain he caused to the she-wolf he mated. With a final glance at Felix's dead body, I turn around and pad back towards the lodge.

Chapter 42 Caden

The crowd dispersed once Grace chased after Felix, the excitement now done, and the crowd needed to prepare to return to their respective packs. Turning to look at my father's body, I let out a sigh and wonder what sort of mess he left me that I will need to sort out. The first task is that a funeral will need to be arranged for him before my coronation can happen.

"I already called a few wolves to come take his body to the morgue." Zander's voice calls out softly, his hand patting my shoulder as he comes to stand next to me. I thank my best friend, realizing that we will also need to have an initiation ceremony to hand over the Beta title to him once we return to the Royal Pack. Caleb and Cody walk over and join us; their faces filled with smiles as they pat me on the back.

"You lucky dog!" Cody chuckles, throwing his arm over my shoulder and pulling me into a side hug.

"That silver she-wolf is one heck of a woman, and you just declared your interest in her just like that? Should I start calling her 'Your Majesty' now?" He continues laughing. I roll my eyes, a smile growing on my face as I think about Grace. Watching her tackle Felix at first made me feel fear. To see the she-wolf I held in my arms hours before as she healed take on my cousin, a well-known woman abuser, worried me to no end. But then I watched her force my cousin to submit, felt the power of an Alpha push through her blood, and I realized that she was defending my honour because she cares about me. It made me happy to think the woman I wanted also wanted me and would defend and protect me just like I would her.

"You just might end up doing that." I chuckle out, getting a look of disbelief from Cody as his arm drops from my shoulder.

"Seems like our King has found his Queen." Caleb states, lightly punching my shoulder. I agree, motioning for the three to follow me as we head to the lodge. A banquet will be prepared for tonight to commemorate the end of The Run this time around, and I will have the be there as the new Alpha King.

"Your Majesty!" A voice calls out, and I turn to see Eli the Ancient walking towards me, a friendly smile on his face. Fangs poke from under his top lip, and part of me heightens my senses as I wait to see what this Vampire wants.

"Lord Eli." I greet, nodding respectfully at the man.

"No need for formalities." Eli brushes me off, a bright smile on his face.

"Let me start off by congratulating you on becoming King. In my opinion, it was about time for Gregory to be put down." Shocked, I take a closer look at Eli and realize he means no harm, and my guard against him lowers. It seems talking to him will be a good thing for me.

"Thank you. I have been debating on how to deal with my father, and death seemed to be the safest option if I want my nation to flourish." I reply back, my own smile mirroring the Vampire's. This seems to be the right thing to say as Eli nods, his eyes scanning the wolves lazing about in the clearing. The Run took a lot out of everyone, and these wolves deserve a relaxing day before we all are to head to our respective packs.

"I came to The Run in order to make a peace treaty with your father, but the man was adamant on not cooperating. I was wondering if, after your coronation, I can come to you and we can come to an alliance. Vampires and Werewolves have been at odds with one another for years. I'd like to see us getting along now that change is around the corner. You and that silver wolf will be bringing a new era to your kind as King and Queen, and I want to be there with you two as a friend." I follow his gaze to see Grace padding towards the Lodge, her silver fur shining in the sun, and I smile. She is the definition of beauty and grace. The perfect woman to bring about change for all. Eli is right, Grace will make a perfect Queen with the compassion and strength she has.

"I'd like that. I will have an invitation sent to you and your coven to come be part of my coronation." Thinking about his words, I extend an offer to Eli. If the two of us can work together, then that will be a good thing. An alliance with the Ancient will be perfect. We can stop many minor conflicts between our races and even open up trade with them.

"We can take the time between now and then to come up with what we expect from one another and finalize the alliance treaty the day after my coronation." Finishing my train of thought, I see the hint of surprise flash in Eli's eyes before it's gone and masked with a friendly diplomatic smile.

"I look forward to that, Caden. Till then, I believe you have some things to take care of." With that, Eli walks away, his steady gait reminding me of a King. I wonder if, through our alliance, Eli can become a mentor to me as I learn how to be a just and fair King.

"We should get things ready for the banquet tonight." Celeb suggests, pulling me from my thoughts. I nod, my friends and I heading inside the lodge only to be greeted by a chaotic scene. Coordinators run about, some carrying trays of food up the stairs where visiting Alphas and Betas stay, some rushing out to the cabins behind the lodge with clean linen, others coming to me asking questions about the meals for the banquet and how to prepare the outside for the final farewell to end The Run. I sigh, looking at Zander, who seems equally frazzled as I am and conclude that we are in for one hell of a night.

With a groan of frustration, I ask the coordinators preparing for the event to step forward and to follow me to the Alpha King's office with Caleb, Cody, Zander, and me. Three wolves step forward, bowing to me respectfully as I lead the way. I can hear my friends snicker about how tough my job of being King will be and that this is a great first step.

Suppressing a growl, I angrily stomp up the stairs and make my way to a solid Oak door with a golden plaque reading *Alpha King's Office* attached to it. Pushing open the door, I make my way to the desk and take a seat on the plush leather chair, the others soon filing in with Zander entering last and closing the door behind him. Once inside, the three wolves preparing the banquet start suggesting ideas all at once, giving me a slight headache.

"Make it a buffet-style dinner." I shout out, silencing the three wolves. They look at me in shock as the banquet has always been a sit-down dinner, but it was time for a change, one I would like to start tonight.

"If we make it a buffet-style dinner, we can give the wolves here a chance to mingle about and get to know their new pack mates as well as form alliances. It will also be easier to create larger portions of food quicker than individual meals, and with the lodge being full of wolves, more food means less angry, quick-to-temper wolves." I explain, the three coordinators taking my words to heart. The female, Leah, if I remember correctly, nods, her eyes glazing over as she mind links someone.

"The chefs like this idea. We can get the rest of the banquet planners to help decorate the outside patio for the buffet." Leah states with an excited grin.

"Sounds good. Leah, you are in charge. Make sure to spread the buffet tables out around the patio so that it is easier to get to the food without long lines."

"Yes, Alpha!" With the banquet problems now settled, the three coordinators leave the office prepared to make the banquet a success. I look to Caleb, who seems to be watching me with amusement written all over his face, and decide that he needs a job to do as well.

"Caleb, since you are just standing there, why not go help Leah move tables." I command, watching the amusement fall from my friend's face.

"What?! Come on, Caden, that's not fair!" He protests, and I wave him off while rummaging through the folders piled high on the right side of the desk. It seems my father brought work with him, work I will need to organize and go through.

"Zander, can you tell my sister to help Grace get ready for the banquet? I plan to bring her as my date." I ask my friend, watching as he smirks and grabs Caleb's arm.

"On it, Alpha. I will bring Caleb to Leah while I am on my way to the medical ward." I nod, happy to have my best friend's support as Zander drags a protesting Caleb out of the office. Looking at Cody, I motion for him to take a seat across from me and hand him a few files, a look of understanding on his face. To think Caleb and he are twins, but are complete polar opposites.

"You went to law school, so I need your help going through some of these. It seems my work as Alpha King has just begun." I state, giving an apologetic smile to my friend.

"It's fine, Caden, I understand." Relieved, the two of us get to work. If I am to make changes, I will need the support of those I call my closest confidants.

Chapter 43 Grace

Entering the medical ward once again, I slink my way towards my room and wonder if my nurse knew I had snuck out. I am careful to avoid the nurses and doctors working and rushing about, not getting in their. As soon as I enter the open door to my assigned room I soon learn that yes, my nurse did indeed know I snuck out as I find her waiting for me in the middle of the room with a frown on her face.

"There are clean clothes in the bathroom for you. Shower and change." She orders, her no-nonsense attitude making me regret worrying her. I nod, slowly walking around Karina and head into the open door of the bathroom. Shifting to my human form, I turn the handles to the small shower on and step into the warm spray. My body is still not at peak strength and fighting Felix had taken a lot out of me. I should have been a little more careful, but when I noticed Caden was gone from my bed, I wanted to find him, to make sure he was safe.

I groan in satisfaction as the hot water pelts against my sore body and lets my thoughts wander to Caden. With him now being the Alpha King, my life will change. I know I have feelings for him, that I want to date him and see where our relationship goes, but I also know that I will be under scrutiny of the many packs as well. I will be a candidate for Alpha Queen and anything I do can result in either a negative or positive response from the people in the werewolf nation.

"Grace, Caden sent orders for me to help you prepare for the banquet. He wants you to be his date." Karina calls out from the other side of the door. I smile and quickly wash my body before taking time to lather my hair and detangle the long locks.

Now clean, I turn the water off, step out of the shower and find a few fluffy towels waiting beside the vanity to be used. Hanging on the wall beside the towels is a clear dress bag with a beautiful sapphire blue sundress carefully placed inside, one that I quickly put on after my body is dried. Throwing the towel in the laundry hamper, I leave the bathroom to find Karina waiting for me with makeup, brushes and a hair drier placed on the little table beside the bed and a large mirror leaning against the wall opposite of a chair.

"How do you like the dress?" she asks making me smile as I look down at the sapphire blue sundress adorned on me.

"I love it. Its very comfortable." I state, nervously smoothing the dress. Karina chuckles, beckoning me to come sit in the chair beside the bed. Walking closer to the she-wolf I take a deep breath and pause – Caden's scent is although faint lingering on her. How did I not notice this.

"How do you know Caden?" I ask, my once friendly tone slowly growing colder as I take a seat. Karina smiles, pulling my damp hair out of the towel turban I had wrapped it into and throwing it to the side.

"He is my half brother." Sensing honesty in her answer, I settle into the chair and relax. Caden did mention a sister when we first got to know each other and I am happy to know that she is the nurse in charge of my care.

Karina then begins to explain that she just turned eighteen a few months ago, making her six years younger than Caden and four years younger than me, and that she was forced to go to the Run, her father hoping to have her mated off to someone soon.

Luckily for Karina she was asked to be a nurse and spent the last seven days learning basic first aid for when the injured would flood in.

"I got lucky. My father was ready to bribe someone into drugging me to make me weak and unable to fight against a male." She sighs out as she places the blow drier down. Reaching over and taking her hand, I give it a small squeeze.

"I'm glad Gregory is dead." I state, turning to see her face light up in a smile.

"So am I." She agrees instantly, her eyes flashing with joy. I chuckle, allowing Karina to do what she wants to me as I wonder about what Caden is doing right now. If he is anxiously waiting to cone fetch me for the banquet and if this will be our first date. Karina is quick with her hands, my hair being twisted and pinned into an intricate bun on top of my head with small braids woven between the strands. I smile at myself in the mirror to see such an elegant hair style on me and wonder if I will have my hair done everyday if I were to mate with Caden. Karina admires her handiwork before stepping in front of me.

"Close your eyes so I can do your makeup." She says quietly, already rummaging through the pallets before her. I chuckle, taking a final look at my hair before closing my eyes. Instantly I feel a brush graze my eye lids, her gentle touch calming as I allow the she-wolf to do as she pleases. A knock at the door sounds and Karina sighs.

"Not done yet!" she yells out, another chuckle coming out of me at the annoyance in her voice.

"Well I would like to take my date to the banquet." Caden's voice argues back, the words slightly muffled by the door. A blush creeps along my face as Karina sighs again, telling me to put the mascara on so she doesn't poke my eyes accidentally. I smile, opening my eyes and taking the mascara wand from her outstretched hand before looking in the mirror. I am shocked by the neutral tones of brown, beige, cream and gold she has paired as my makeup, my sapphire eyes popping with the muted colours. I accepts the lash curler from Karina, quickly finishing the look with mascara and take a final look at myself.

"Very regal looking." Karina states matter-of-factly, making me turn to see her holding a pair of black flats out to me. I thank her, taking the shoes and slipping them on.

"I think you should open the door and allow my brother to bask in your beauty." She nudges my shoulder with her own, a playful smirk on her face. My blush deepens but I agree, making my way closer to the door. Taking a deep breath, I turn the handle and pull the door open, coming face to face with Caden who stares wide eyed at me, a soft smile on his face.

Chapter 44 Caden

─────

S taring at Grace before me, her face pink with a blush, I can't help but reach out and graze the back of my hand along her soft cheek.

"Beautiful." I whisper out, getting a shy smile as a response from her. She mumbles a soft thank you, and for a moment, I enjoy this shy side of her. She has been nothing but a strong, independent she-wolf before me since we met. Only shedding tears when needed. It is rare to see her this shy and quiet, and I think this side makes her quite adorable.

"Okay, love birds, the banquet needs you to make an appearance Caden." Karina interjects, coming to stand behind Grace as she sends me a smirk. I roll my eyes at my sister, deciding that ignoring the feisty she-wolf is best, before holding my hand out to Grace.

"Shall we?" I ask, smiling as Grace places her hand in mine, giving me an equally large smile.

"We shall!" she answers, her sapphire eyes sparkling and allowing me to lead her from her room in the medical ward and out of the building. The music for the banquet can be heard from the entrance of the building, and I slow my steps, not ready to deal with the other wolves just yet. I want to savour this alone time with Grace before we are surrounded by wolves from all over the world.

"If we go any slower, the banquet will be over." Grace chuckles, pressing herself against my arm. I sigh, knowing she is right, and pull her in for a hug.

"Is it bad that I want to avoid everything and just sneak off?" I ask, smiling as she snuggles closer into my embrace, resting her head against my shoulder.

"As much as I agree with you and want to sneak off, we need to go to the banquet since you are now the King." She reasons, making me sigh once more. Grace is right as always. As King, I need to make an appearance at the banquet and announce plans for when The Run returns in six months. Groaning in frustration, I place a quick kiss on Grace's lips before we continue walking towards the other side of the lodge, where a large patio waits. Rounding the corner, I am in awe at how fast the coordinators have worked with the patio being set with multiple tables full of food and seating areas arranged around the clearing.

The grassy lawn in front of the patio is filled with wolves mingling with one another as a D.J. set up on the far-right side of the lawn plays upbeat music. As soon as wolves notice me, they begin to bow, backing away to give Grace and me room to move. Word of my arrival must have spread as the music stops and silence reigns while Grace and I stand in the middle of the patio, all eyes on us.

"Long live the King!" Someone shouts after an uncomfortable silence settles over everyone. Soon, another wolf chimes in, then another until the crowd is chanting *Long Live the King*. Grace chuckles beside me, nudging my shoulder playfully with hers as she also chants along. My right eye twitches in annoyance, but I realize I will soon need to become accustomed to this reaction as my reign has just begun. I raise my hand into the air, signalling for silence, and wait for the wolves to settle once more.

"Hello, everyone, and welcome to the final banquet." I greet, getting a cheer from the crowd once more. Suppressing a groan, I begin wondering if everyone will be this excitable whenever I want to make an announcement.

"Settle down, everyone!" Grace orders, her smile set into a playful smirk. She is clearly enjoying my discomfort. As the crowd quiets again, I thank her before turning back to face the crowd.

"I want to apologize for my behaviour earlier today, but I also want to assure you all that killing my father was the right thing to do. As such, I want to announce that The Run, which is to happen in six months, will be cancelled to give our people time to mourn and to become accustomed to my reign." I begin to explain, seeing confusion and shock amongst the crowd.

"So does that mean we won't be able to find mates?" Someone asks. Unsure what to do, I turn to look at Grace, who gives me an encouraging smile. I know what needs to be done if I want to make Grace my mate and Queen in the near future.

"No, you can still find mates." I answer, smiling at the crowd as I pull Grace closer to my side.

"For the next six months and as long as it is consensual, you and your partner can complete the mate bond without having to go into The Run." I proclaim, seeing excitement on everyone's face.

"Does that mean we can mate with our boyfriend or girlfriend?" A she-wolf asks in excitement. I smile, realizing it is Amelia calling out from the crowd, her arms wrapped around her boyfriend, Bryden.

"Yes. You can do so as soon as you'd like." I confirm seeing a look of gratitude in my friend's eyes. This seems to be all she needs, and I have a feeling I will be attending a wedding in a few weeks.

"In the meantime, I will be making changes to the laws that govern our nation, as well as giving she-wolves their rights as strong members of our race. Enjoy the last banquet of The Run as I plan to make significant changes going forward." With that, I guide Grace to one of the buffet tables and hand her a plate. The music resumes and the happy atmosphere returns as Grace and I choose what to eat. Amelia and Bryden soon join us, the blonde giving me a quick hug, thanking me for the opportunity for her and Bryden to finally mate one another, and introducing me to the man himself.

"Thank you for protecting Amelia." Bryden smiles at me as I shake his hands, surprising me with how calm this soon-to-be Alpha wolf is.

"No need to thank me." I brush off his thanks with a smile and pull Grace to my side, watching as she scoops a forkful of potato salad into her mouth.

"Hungry?" I ask, placing a kiss on her forehead. She nods, not bothering to answer me as she continues to eat her food, and Amelia gives me a helpless look.

"You might want to fill another two plates for her before she is ready to talk." The blonde sighs, shaking her head at Grace, who rolls her eyes and sticks her tongue out at Amelia. I chuckle, deciding to find an empty table for the four of us to sit at that is close to the buffet spread and easily find one within seconds. As soon as we take a seat, Zander and Karina quickly join us, my sister carrying two plates full of food while Zander watches her with concern.

"I have a feeling we may need more food for the banquet." My Beta states as Karina sits beside Grace, the two she-wolves nodding a greeting before they silently eat.

"I have a feeling you are right." I laugh out as Karina offers Grace a kabob from one of her plates, and Grace, in turn, shares a piece of corn bread. It seems these two really hit it off.

Introducing the two wolves that are family to me to Bryden and Amelia, I am happy to see Zander and Bryden instantly hit it off right away as the two begin discussing cross-training with our warriors. Amelia and Karina begin to talk about my coronation, what outfit the girls will wear and what colour scheme they should have, as I notice Grace's plate soon becoming empty. Placing a soft kiss on her cheek, I stand and promise to return as I go up to the buffet table once more and fill another plate of food for Grace and me, bringing it to the table just as she finishes her first, earning myself a not-so-chaste kiss on the lips as thanks. Note to self, find out what food Grace likes to make for her in the future.

"Seems our little family is getting along." I whisper into her ear as she takes a sip of water, wrapping my arm around her shoulder.

"Seems like they are." Grace agrees, a smile on her face. Looking out to the crowd of dancing and mingling wolves, I sigh and wonder just what I am going to do to replace The Run by next year.

"Penny for your thoughts?" Grace asks, drawing my attention back to her as she pushes her now empty plate away and scoots her chair closer to me.

"I'm thinking about how next year there The Run will be no more." I answer, my emerald eyes looking into her sapphire ones. She smiles, turning to look at the crowd of wolves as newly mated pairs dance and those still single mingle about. Many will be leaving for their new packs with their mates tomorrow, some even moving to new countries.

"That would be a dream come true for a lot of she-wolves." She whispers, and I nod in agreement, thinking about the work ahead of me.

"But what will replace The Run?" Her question has me frowning, and I can't help but sigh as I look away from her, towards the forest bathed in the blue moonlight.

"I am not sure yet." I answer honestly, running my free hand through my hair as Bryden takes Amelia to dance and Zander rushes after a now drunk Karina, the wolf more of a worrywart to her than I am.

"But I am sure you and I can come up with a great idea that will benefit every wolf." I continue, turning to catch the surprised look on her face. My instinct tells me that Grace is the one I am meant to be with, to have as a co-ruler of all wolves and that if these last seven days have taught me anything, it's that as long as I have Grace beside me, I know everything will work out in the end. Her brilliant mind will be able to help create an event that would benefit everyone in the werewolf nation and be fair for the she-wolves to attend.

Chapter 45 Grace

⸻

"Damn it, Grace, just sit still already!" Amelia growls out as I turn to look at the clock to check the time for the umpteenth time. She takes my head in her hands and forces me to face the mirror once more, her blue eyes staring at me with annoyance as Bryden chuckles from the couch against the wall.

"I'm sorry, but he should have been here by now!" I state, slightly pouting as I wait for Caden to arrive. It has been exactly six months since Caden and I had our first date, and the nation is celebrating not having to participate in the Run last week. As promised, many she-wolves were able to find their own mate as well, and those who chose to absolve their bonds were able to do so with the Council's help.

A lot has changed in the last six months, from Caden and me falling in love, to Amelia being mated to Bryden and now two months pregnant with their first pup, to Karina, Zander, Cody, and me helping Caden with revising werewolf laws. Amelia and Bryden are now the Alpha of Silver Birch, and I am their Beta – for now, that is. Our fathers stepped down from their positions as per Amelia's father's and I's bet. Now they live their lives as Omegas, unable to interfere with pack politics.

"Caden will be here when he said he would be here. Right now, I need to finish your make-up." My pregnant friend sighs in exasperation, giving me a glare when I try to move once more. Sitting still, I allow her to finish her handiwork, deciding that pissing off a pregnant she-wolf any further is not a good idea. Besides, instinct tells me she and Bryden have been hiding something from me about tonight.

"There, done. And about time too." Amelia declares as she steps to the right and allows me to see myself in the mirror. Staring wide-eyed at my reflection, I tentatively touch the loose silver curls cascading down my back, my hair surprisingly soft while still maintaining its shape. My make-up is done in neutral tones, the soft creams and browns matching the flowy cream sweetheart neckline dress I was forced to wear.

"You look perfect for what Caden has planned!" She giggles out, flopping onto the couch beside her mate. I roll my eyes at her, already knowing that she will ignore my question if I ask what Caden has planned for the night, and instead slip my feet into the silver heels.

On our first date after the banquet, Caden had taken me out for a picnic by a lake during sunset, the two of us relishing in the alone time together. We had lain on the blanket by the bank of the water, the breeze cool on my skin, and watched as fireflies floated above the water. We took the time to really get to know one another without the threat of other wolves looming over us and a deadline to make, and I learned that the food in the picnic basket was made by him.

"Hello?" I smile as Caden's voice calls out from downstairs, bringing me out of my thoughts.

"Upstairs, Caden!" Amelia calls out, giving me a playful wink. The door to my room soon opens, and I smile as I turn around to see my boyfriend striding in wearing a pair of dress slacks and a navy dress shirt.

"Hey, Caden." Amelia greets, standing from the couch and tugging at Bryden's hand.

"Hey, Amelia." He greets back as Bryden chuckles, standing from his spot on the couch and walking over to his friend, giving Caden a fist bump while Amelia is pulled in for a hug.

"Enjoy your date, you two, see you in the morning Grace." Bryden says with a mischievous smile as Amelia starts to drag him out of the room. I roll my eyes at the two, deciding that whatever they are not telling me will be well worth the wait. The door shuts behind them as I stand, only to feel strong arms pull me into a familiar embrace. Caden's lips are on mine in seconds, his hand cupping the back of my head as he deepens the kiss. I moan, my eyes fluttering shut while our tongues fight for dominance until we have no choice but to pull away breathless.

"You look stunning, Lady Silver." He whispers once we pull away, his thumb caressing my swollen lips.

"And you look incredible." My voice is a whisper as I look into his eyes, seeing them reflect so much love back at me. To think I went into the Run determined not to be mated and found the love of my life.

"Let's head out, shall we?" He whispers, and I smile with excitement. His lips graze mine once more in a gentle kiss before he takes my hand. We quickly leave my room, heading down the stairs of the pack house and greeting the few pack members lingering in the halls.

Ever since Amelia had taken over, Silver Birch has expanded with new wolves wanting to join. Some came because they learned that I -the Alpha King's girlfriend - am the Beta, while others wanted to live in a pack ruled by a fair and just Alpha pair.

My Alpha blood from my mother's side awakened soon after I accepted Caden as mine, and our love for one another grew. It got to the point that Amelia and I sometimes find it hard to be near each other with such strong blood coursing through both our veins, but we learned to cope with the situation as she trained me to run a pack and I trained her soon-to-be Beta, Leah. We both knew that sooner or later I would move to Caden's pack and become the next Alpha Queen, and that my short role as her Beta would come to an end. It is bittersweet to think that I will be leaving her here one day, but Caden is King, and my heart goes where he goes.

"You okay?" Caden asks, sensing my shifting mood as we exit the pack house, me looking back at it as a bitter sadness fills me.

"Yes. I was just thinking how one day this place will no longer be my home." I answer with a small smile, linking my arms around his right arm.

"Why do you say that?" He asks, worry in his voice.

"Because one day I will be mated to you and your Queen. Where you are is where my home will be." Surprise flickers in his eyes, and I wonder if he also thought about this. Giving him a reassuring smile, I place a kiss on his cheek as we make our way to his truck.

"So where are we going?" I ask as he helps me climb into the passenger side, a smirk on his face when he takes my hand and places a kiss on it.

"That is a surprise, my Lady Silver." He whispers with a wink before closing the door and making his way to the driver's side. He climbs in, making sure that both our seatbelts are on before turning the key and driving away. The radio is playing softly, and as a song I know comes on, I sing along. Caden just smiles beside me, his fingers tapping along to the beat as my voice carries around us.

After a few songs, the cabin fills with a comfortable silence, trees passing by us, and the scent of the forest rushing in on the wind. The car finally comes to a stop, my head turning to face Caden just as his lips descend onto my own. It's a slow and steady kiss that melts my heart. His hands hold me gently while mine clutch at his shirt.

"I love you, Grace." He whispers when we pull away, foreheads pressed together as we catch our breaths from another long kiss.

"I love you too, Caden," I whisper back, resting my head against his shoulder and listening to his steady heartbeat. I wish we could stay here and just relax in the truck as we have done many times already, but Caden reminds me I have yet to see my surprise before climbing out of the truck, makes his way to my side and helps me out of the truck. He takes my hand, asking me to keep my eyes closed so that I do not see the surprise early, and guiding me safely towards the sound of the lake.

Chapter 46 Caden

———

"You can open your eyes now." I mumble out, my eyes never leaving Grace's face as her eyes slowly open. I watch as her face goes from one filled with smiles to one of shock and disbelief as she takes in the crystal-clear lake in front of us with a small sailboat bobbing gently on the waves.

"Is that a boat?" She gasps out in surprise, her head moving to look at me, then the boat, then back at me. I chuckle, finding her adorable and wrapping my arms around her from behind, pulling her towards my chest. Resting my head on her shoulder, I place a kiss on the crook of her neck where my mark will one day be before deciding to answer her.

"Yes, Grace, that is a boat." I whisper close to her ear, feeling her shiver. I can feel her excitement to climb onto and explore the boat, a boat that I have a feeling she will be spending a lot of time on. Goddess, I love this woman so much, but maybe buying her a boat was a bad idea.

"Would my Princess like to take a cruise on the Lady Silver?" I ask, moving to stand in front of Grace as I offer her my hand. She takes it, her brows furrowed as I inwardly sigh.

"You named a boat after me!" She exclaims in annoyance, frowning as I lead her towards the small sailboat.

"Caden, what did I say about -" She continues, and I can already tell a lecture is on the tip of her tongue. Without thinking, I pull her into my arms and capture her lips with mine, a heated kiss ensuing. Any protest she might have had is gone as her eyes flutter close and she melts into my arms, her lips moving just as frantically as mine move. As our kiss comes to an end, I smile at her slightly dazed look and blushing cheeks before placing a gentle kiss on her forehead.

"Yes, I named a boat after you, and I know you hate it when I name things after you in any way." I begin to explain, watching as her misty eyes slowly turn into slits as she glares at me.

"But since this is your boat. You can rename it Grace." My statement is said calmly, and I smirk as I watch her shocked expression take over. I grin as she looks towards the boat once more, then back at me, then at the boat again, feeling a small victory in my heart as she pulls away from my embrace to step close to the boat.

"This is mine?" She asks in a small whisper as she runs her hand along the side, a smile on her lips.

"It's yours Grace." I confirm, slowly walking towards her as she studies the small sailboat.

"Now you can go sailing whenever you want and go swimming in the ocean. That is after we move the boat." I continue, pulling her into my arms once again and poking her nose. She giggles, the sound causing my heart to quicken. Getting to know her and her pack, I have learned that Grace is usually the strong, stoic type. Her packmates quickly learned how capable a Beta she is, always solving problems as they arise with Amelia. They are a formidable pair, and if I weren't the Alpha King, I would be her support as the Beta under Bryden. It isn't until she is alone with those she considers family that the childlike innocence in her comes out. When she laughs and giggles like a regular twenty-year-old she-wolf instead of a scowling Beta.

Her eyes continue to study the ship, and I think back to our first date when she explained how she spent her summer days in her maternal family's pack – Ocean Heart – with her grandfather. Fishing at sea and swimming in the ocean. Her goal is to one day own a boat of her own where she can sail to her heart's content. To know I made one of her goals happen makes me happy to be hers.

"Would you like to board the ship, Captain Grace?" I ask, watching her eyes widen in excitement.

"Yes, I would!" She excitedly answers, pulling away from my embrace to rush to the back of the boat where a small platform sits just above the water. I hold out my hand to help steady her as she leaps onto the platform, but she surprises me by landing gracefully close to the edge, her heels barely hindering her steps, and I watch as she ascends the steps.

With a chuckle, I follow suit and carefully leap onto the platform where she once stood, following her up the steps and smiling when I see her standing before the large banquet with multiple pillows for comfort set with dining wear set up for two and a picnic basket and a bottle of wine sitting in an ice bucket sitting in the middle waiting to be opened. Quietly padding till I am behind her, I slowly lower myself onto one knee and take out the box that has been in my pocket all day, one that holds my mother's ring that Amelia helped me size to fit Grace.

"Caden, this is increda-" She stops mid-sentence as she turns around, her sapphire eyes once again wide with shock and surprise. I smile sheepishly, my heart fluttering as she looks at the ring box in my hand. Taking a deep breath to settle my nerves, her scent of lavender and mint wraps around me, reminding me that this is the woman I want to belong to.

"Grace." I begin, looking into her eyes that are already filling with tears.

"Will you-"

Chapter 47 Grace

———

Staring down at Caden kneeling before me with the dainty diamond and sapphire ring, the one I have seen many times in portraits of his mother, twinkling in the moonlight, I feel tears welling in my eyes. To think, six months ago, I did not want to find a mate in The Run. That I did not want to have a partner unless it was someone I truly loved. Now here I am with a man I met in The Run that I want to be with for the rest of my life.

"Grace." His voice is husky, filled with emotions, and I spy his eyes slowly growing glassy with tears as well.

"Will you..." He trails off, taking a deep breath and closing his eyes for a moment. I can smell his nervousness in the air, hear the quickening of his heartbeat, and know that no matter what, I will always say yes to this man as long as he has the courage to ask. His emerald eyes open and stare into mine as love, love for me, is clearly displayed in those gem-like eyes.

"Grace, My Princess and the love of my life. Will you marry me? Will you share my life with me and be mine?" His voice cracks mid-sentence as he fights back tears, and my own begin to flow. I feel my legs shake as an overwhelming happiness washes over me.

"Grace?" Caden asks, his voice holding a hint of worry and fear. I lower myself onto my knees and allow myself to cry harder, unable to put into words how happy I am.

Happy that a man wants me for me.

Happy I found my soul mate in Caden.

Happy that I did not kill him the first day I met him, thinking he was trying to rape Amelia.

Thank you, Amelia, for stopping me from ruining my future.

"Grace, I'm sorry if this is too fast!" Panic rises into Caden's voice as he lowers the hand holding the ring box while his free hand reaches out to wipe away my tears as best as he can. Guilt for making him worry wells inside me, but the happiness overpowers it.

"I'm sorry, I just-" I sob out, still unable to form words. Without thinking, I wrap my arms around his neck and pull him towards me, pouring all my love and emotions into a kiss. His arms wrap around me, pulling my body flush against him as our lips dance with each other once again. My tears slow as I think about all the happy moments we have had since meeting, all the sad moments that made me realize I have grown feelings for him, but most importantly, all the moments that made me realize I am utterly in love with this wolf before me. Sadly, he pulls away from me as we soon become breathless, leaving us panting heavily as I look at him, still crying.

"Yes." I manage to whisper out, smiling at Caden as I wipe away some more tears.

"What?" He asks, confused, and I realized I had whispered too quietly to hear.

"Yes! Yes, I'll marry you! I'll be yours and you'll be mine!" I exclaim as I cry harder, feeling him pull me to his chest as I bury my face into the crook of his neck, inhaling his calming scent.

"You will?" He asks hopefully, and I nod.

"Yes." I laugh as he pulls away to hold me at arm's length, amazement in his eyes. He is such a dork at times, but he is my dork.

"I love you, Grace." He says as he pulls me into his embrace once more, his face burying into my hair and inhaling my scent deeply.

"I love you too, Caden," I reply back, wiping away more tears. Six months ago, all I wanted was to avoid The Run and help my pack mates to be able to choose whether or not they wanted to go to the event. I wanted freedom to find my own love and live my life free from the anxiety of being raped and claimed by some unknown power-hungry male. Being forced to go led me to Caden. Led me to a life where I can be loved and love back. To a life I can bring change. My love for Caden is something I never thought would be possible, but now I will do everything I can to keep this love for the rest of our lives.

Chapter 48 Caden

———

I watch Grace as she sleeps, the ring now placed on her left ring finger, gleaming in whatever light filters in from the porthole. She clutches the blanket covered in our scent, and I smile. This she-wolf is mine, and I am hers. Letting out a soft sigh, I think about the future we will have, a future as King and Queen with pups of our own one day. But something bothers me.

We have been able to avoid continuing the Run this time with all the new changes taking place over the last six months, but now we have to plan for the next one that is supposed to take place in another six months' time. I have yet to find a substitute that will prevent senseless raping of she-wolves and allow the women of our nation a chance to actually find love like Grace and I did. We could probably use our engagement as an excuse to cancel the next one, but what about the one after that and the one after that? We need to find a permanent solution and soon.

"Caden?" Her sleepy voice fills the cabin, pulling me from my thoughts. Seeing her sleepy gaze and outstretched arms beckoning me to return to her side, I walk back to the bed, climb under the blankets and pull Grace on top of me, her hands instantly clinging to me as she buries her face in the crook of my neck. We agreed that the day she moves into the palace, we will complete the mating in our home. For now, she kisses the spot her mark will one day be placed.

"Sorry, I couldn't sleep." I whisper as I inhale her scent, fingers gently combing through her hair.

"Wanna tell me what's wrong?" She yawns halfway through her question, and I chuckle, placing a soft kiss on her temple. Goddess, I love this woman.

"Not right now." I answer, hearing her yawn once again as she snuggles closer.

"You just go back to sleep, my Princess." She nods against my chest after I say this, her breath evening out as she goes back to sleep, and I smile again. I am lucky to have met her, and now I need to be the Alpha King she believes me to be. I just hope she can handle the stress of The Crown when the time comes.

About the Author

Born and raised in Brampton, Ontario - also known as "The Flower City"- Alana Dyer started her relationship with books on a "Hate/Hate" relationship as a child that quickly became a passion for reading as she found that novels can bring you places never seen before.

From finding her love of reading, Alana Dyer soon began writing little stories as a child, and in 2015, with the discovery of Wattpad, Alana started writing seriously with the hopes of one day publishing. Five years later, after writing for a loyal fanbase, Alana debuted on August 30th, 2020, on Amazon with her first full-length novel, "The Runaway Breeder".

Now in 2023, Alana Dyer has published 6 novels and two Novelettes under the pen name A. Dyer and spends her days writing, playing with her many pets and planning to expand the distribution of her books.

Rejection Series

Three she-wolves learn that life can take a turn for the worst and those who are supposed to love you can become your worst enemies. When the Moon Goddess and fate play a cruel card that shatters each of their hearts and a budding war is on the horizon can each one find their true strength that lie within and figure out just who is the mastermind in the war that will change the fate of the werewolf race?

Follow Amberle and her Full Moon Rejection in "Rejection on the Full Moon"

See if Geminie's soul mate regrets "Rejecting the Future Moon Goddess"

Can "Rejection to the Alpha King's Daughter" bring out the true Werewolf Queen in Crystalline

And will these girls be able to piece together the true Soulless Evil that hides behind his War?

Rejection on the Full Moon

Book 1

SOULLESS - WEREWOLVES who have turned rogue with no humanity left, giving in to their beastly urges.

Rejection - an act in which your soulmate rejects the mate bond, causing immense pain to the rejected.

These are the challenges Amberle Crest must overcome after becoming an outcast amongst the wolves her age due to an event outside of her control.

When her mate rejects her on her eighteenth birthday, Amberle realizes that living in a pack where the majority would rather use her as a slave than treat her as an equal is not worth the pain. She becomes the notorious wolf, Fire Foot, vowing that everyone would regret how they treated her, as she leaves her pack in the past.

Now a ghost forgotten by those that tormented her, Amberle does whatever it takes to survive as a lone wolf. A fateful day changes her lonely life to one full of happiness and hope—until ghosts from her own past call for aid in ridding their pack of the Soulless who threatens all wolf kind.

Faced with new friends, old foes, and the threat of a building army, will Amberle be able to fight the ghosts of her past to cherish the pack she has found or will an old mate claim her before a second chance mate can show her what being treasured by someone is all about?

Rejecting the Future Moon Goddess

Book 2

Soulless - werewolves who have turned rogue with no humanity left, giving in to their beastly urges.

Rejection - an act in which your soulmate rejects the mate bond, causing immense pain to the rejected.

Moon Goddess - the deity that created the werewolf race whom her creation worship

Omega - The lowest ranked wolf in the pack sometimes treated as nothing more than a slave or an object

These are the things Geminie Blake learns after being blamed for the tragic Deaths of her Alpha and Luna. With the pack turned against her and failing to shift as a wolf, Geminie faces challenges every day with the hope of one day gaining freedom or her mate saving her. But when her fated soul mate ends up being her ex-best friend and the son to the late Alpha and Luna rejects her, Geminie's life changes drastically.

Learning that she is not Geminie Blake - daughter to the Beta couple - but Geminie Starlite - daughter to the Moon Goddess and Future Moon Goddess herself - Geminie quickly faces the new challenges thrown her way as she navigates her wolf form and Goddess powers, creating a pack that rivals that of Blood Moon and building her life from scratch to one day take up the mantel as Moon Goddess becomes her priority.

Now, thriving and loving herself for who she is, Geminie forces the past behind her as she waits for her second chance at love. When her first mate requests help and aid from a threat created by Soulless and a potential Leader of the wolves that have lost their Humanity, Geminie is forced to face the wounds left unhealed and return to the place she called hell for eleven years of her life.

Will Geminie be able to overcome the scars left by years of abuse and find love once and for all, or will the panful wounds of her past and threat from the Leader of the army of Soulless ready to kill at a moments notice take the last bit of happiness this young Goddess has left.

Rejection to the Alpha King's Daughter

Book 3

Soulless - werewolves who have turned rogue with no humanity left, giving in to their beastly urges.

Rejection - an act in which your soulmate rejects the mate bond, causing immense pain to the rejected.

Moon Goddess - the deity that created the werewolf race whom her creation worship

Omega - The lowest ranked wolf in the pack sometimes treated as nothing more than a slave or an object

Alpha King/Queen - The rulers of the werewolf nation

Runt - The smallest of the wolf pack, usually ignored or bullied for being the smallest

Crystalline Thorn grows under the abuse by her father as she trains to take the throne one day and become the Alpha Queen, leader of every wolf in the werewolf nation. She dreams of the day when she meets her mate and be accepted as a strong Queen, especially since she is a runt.

But her dream is soon shattered when on the day of an Alliance her mate discovers her "weak" form and rejects her promptly leading to her father disowning her and her hopes to inherit the throne is dashed. But that is the least of her worries. Soon, with the help of Geminie and Amberle, Crystalline learns of a war that has been brewing for thousands of years, of a destiny that has been written in the stars by the original Moon Goddess - Luna - and the Goddess of Destiny - Morai - have placed upon her and her connection to the Lost Princess.

Will Crystalline be able to retrieve her throne?

Will she accept the mate that rejected her or chose the second chance mate?

Or will the weight of responsibility handed to her crush her entirely?

Books by the Author

CONTACT THE AUTHOR

 alana.dyer.author@
hotmail.com

 author.alana.dyer

 alana.dyer

 Alana Dyer
@alana.dyer.author

E-BOOK | PAPERBACK | HARDCOVERS
available where books are sold

Don't miss out!

Visit the website below and you can sign up to receive emails whenever Alana Dyer publishes a new book. There's no charge and no obligation.

https://books2read.com/r/B-A-LXGX-HMDOC

BOOKS 2 READ

Connecting independent readers to independent writers.